A CLASSIC CHINESE READER

# MASTERS ON MASTERPIECES OF SONG LYRICS

COMPILED
BY EDITORIAL BOARD
OF CHINESE LITERATURE AND HISTORY

TRANSLATED BY ZHU JIANTING AND ZHAO GUOYA

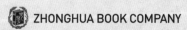 CHINA INTERCONTINENTAL PRESS    ZHONGHUA BOOK COMPANY

# A Bleak and Solemn Bugle Call in the Frontier
## – On the *Pride of Fishermen* by Fan Zhongyan

Ma Maoyuan, Wang Congren

### Tune: Pride of Fishermen

*When autumn comes to the frontier, the scene looks drear;*
*Southbound wild geese won't stay e'en for a day.*
*An uproar rises with horns blowing far and near.*
*Walled in by peaks, smoke rises straight*
*At sunset over isolate town with closed gate.*

*I hold a cup of wine, yet home is far away;*
*The northwest not yet won, I can't but stay.*

*At the flutes' doleful sound over frost-covered ground,*
*None falls asleep;*
*The general's hair turns white and soldiers weep.*

Fan Zhongyan (989-1052), a renowned politician and essayist in the Northern Song Dynasty, was also an outstanding lyricist. Only six of his lyrics are passed on to today including the aforesaid *Pride of Fishermen* as the most popular one.

From the first year of the Kangding Period under the reign of Emperor Renzong of the Song Dynasty (1040), Fan Zhongyan had served as the deputy general of Shaanxi cum magistrate of Yanzhou (Today's Yan'an, Shaanxi) and garrisoned the frontier for four years. The lyric is a reflective creation of Fan during his northwestern service years.

The first stanza describes the autumn scenery in the frontier region. In the first line, the diction "different" is of great importance. It indicates both the scenic difference between the frontier and the central plains and the changes of frontier scenery in autumn and rolls out the scenic description in this stanza.

In the south of Hengyang, Hunan province stands the Huiyan Peak which is the termination of the birds' southward migration. Although migration is an intuition, the lyricist personified it in the line "Southbound wild geese won't stay e'en for a day" to describe his own feeling.

The next three lines present the desolation of the frontier region. The "uproar" refers to the bleak sound only heard in the frontier. In *The Letter to Su Wu* written on the name of Li Ling, the lines "Listen attentively, you may hear the uproar arise: the sound of Hu Jia (a reed instrument), the neigh of horses and the cry of animals" are good explanations to the line "an uproar rises with horns blowing far and near." The uproar, together with the bugle call of the barracks, creates a bleak and solemn atmosphere. "Walled in by peaks, smoke rises straight; At sunset over isolate town with closed gate" are descriptions of an extremely desolate and majestic frontier fortress. Countless peaks stand steadily like protection walls. At sunset, amid the peaks lies an isolate town with its gate tightly closed. The skillful application of nouns and verbs in the three lines vivifies the intense situation in the frontier town.

The second stanza turns from scenery description to emotion expression. A cup of wine can never extinguish the fire of nostalgia, but intensifies the homesickness. However, the reason for the garrison is "The northwest

The Portrait of Fan Zhongyan

3

not yet won, I can't but stay." In 89, General Dou Xian attacked the Northern Huns and erected a tablet to mark his victory. This line quotes the history to explain the reason and the lyricist's contradictory and complicated mood.

Actually, Fan Zhongyan took the office of the magistrate of Yanzhou just because of his enthusiastic patriotism. In 1039, Zhao Yuanhao betrayed the Song Dynasty and established Western Xia. In 1040, the Western Xia attacked Yanzhou, besieged the city for seven days and captured the major generals. The besieged city was overwhelmed by depression. Coincidentally, a heavy snow forced the invaders to withdraw and saved the city. But the cowardly officials fled away from the city. Zhang Cunjiu, the new magistrate of Yanzhou, demanded to be transferred to the central plains due to "having no knowledge on militarism" and "caring for his elderly parents." So, Fan had to stand up and voluntarily shouldered the defense responsibility. He hoped to overturn the disadvantages and permanently end the warfare. However, it was impossible for him to become a successful hero like General Dou Xian in a militarily weak dynasty like the Northern Song. The collision between Fan's dream and the objective reality reached the culmination. So, at the flutes' doleful sound on a frosty, sleepless night, the general (referring to Fan himself) and the soldiers fell into a deep sorrow over the country's fate and shed tears of homesickness.

Yanran Mountain

The tune of *Pride of Fishermen* shows a depressive and gloomy atmosphere, brings reader an indignant and melancholy mood, which is determined by the historical period and political environment. During the period under the reign of Emperor Renzong of the Song Dynasty, the country seemed stable superficially but the threat of Liao and Western Xia had kept on rising. But the Song court had dragged out an ignoble existence and continued the stifling status which was quite different from the thriving Tang and the ethnic contradiction-intensive transitional period from the Northern Song to the Southern Song. After assuming the office in Yanzhou, Fan built fortresses, drilled the soldiers, comforted the sufferers and contacted ethnic groups. The Western Xia's aristocracy was frightened by his actions and said "Fan is equivalent to tens of thousands soldiers." However, Fan could only make passive defense and had no possibility to recapture the lost land. The lyric gives a vague reflection of the gloomy era.

Starting from scratch, Fan rolled out intense struggle with the decrepit gerentocratic force after being appointed by the court. According to the *History of the Song Dynasty*, Fan had been politically progressive and "dashed ahead regardless of his safety for the good of the people." However, before the Reform by Wang Anshi, the big bureaucrats and landlords controlled the court, and the officials from middle- and lower-class were disadvantageous in the struggle. So, the struggle of Fan

The Site of Fan Dike in Yancheng, Jiangsu Province

and his peers were vulnerable and powerless, which adds somberness and sentimentalism to his lyrics.

As an ambitious feudal official, Fan was a hero influenced by the spirit of "Can a soldier remain at home while the Huns are still undefeated?" But in face of the hard times, he also had a depressive feeling. Thus, a complicated and special contradiction was produced in his inner heart, which is also exhibited in the lyric: his concern about the reality causes indignation and discontent, and the limitation of the class and era he belonged to produces desolation and depression. The unification of these two factors creates a unique style of Fan's lyrics.

The tune of the *Pride of Fishermen* is quite different from the high-spirited Frontier Poetry of the prosperous Tang Dynasty, for instance the *Army Life (IV)* by Wang Changling says:

> *Clouds on frontier o'ershadow mountains clad in snow;*
> *A lonely town afar faces Pass of Jade Gate.*
> *Our golden armor pierced by sand, we fight the foe;*
> *We won't come back till we destroy the hostile state.*

Both works described the desolate frontier, the isolated town, and the patriotism of the garrison soldiers. Fan quoted the anecdote of Dou Xian while Wang borrowed the story of Fu Jiezi who plotted the assassination of the King of Loulan and opened the communication between the Han Court and the Western Regions. The theme of the two works is completely the same. However, Fan couldn't show the confidence in victory like Wang because he lived in a totally different times.

Despite that, the *Pride of Fishermen* is an outstanding patriotic work which expresses the intensive emotion of resisting foreign invasion and making contributions to the motherland.

Poems and lyrics were distinctive literature styles in ancient China. Poems were composed for expressing ambitions and reflecting realities while lyrics were created for recreation and romance. The tradition had been continued to the early years of Northern Song. This lyric by Fan was a great breakthrough and initiated the Frontier Lyrics School. Later on, Su Shi, Xin Qiji and other lyricists promoted this style and expanded the themes. So, the *Pride of Fishermen* is also of great importance in the development history of lyrics.

# Two Lyrics of Zhang Xian

Cai Yijiang

Zhang Xian (990-1178), alias Ziye, was a native of Wucheng (Today's Wuxing, Zhejiang). He was a renowned lyricist in the early years of the Northern Song and equally famous with another lyricist Liu Yong. His best-known lines include "flowers show beautiful shadows when the moon comes out from clouds," "flower shadows passing through curtains," and "shadows of willow catkin are evasive." His works are collected in the *Anlu Lyrics (An Lu Ci)* including the two noted ones as follows.

**Tune: Lyrics to a Tippler's Drooping Whip**

*Embroidered with a pair of butterflies was her dress,*
*It was at a banquet by the East Pond, when we first met.*
*With only a lightly powdered and rouged face,*
*She was a flower at ease in spring, delicate and dainty.*

*Everything about her on close looks was fair.*
*Everyone spoke praise of her willowy waist.*
*Yesterday she seemed like someone from uninhabited*
*hills at sunset,*
*Tinged all over with vivid clouds as she came.*

The lyric seems like a portrait of a young and beautiful girl. Different from a portrait, it is a vivid and dynamic depiction.

The lyric has a clear structure, starting from clothing (a dress with a pair of butterflies), then cosmetics (lightly powdered and rouged face) and body (willowy waist), and finally demeanor (a fairy amid clouds). In terms of time sequence, the lyric begins with the first sight, then the second look to highlight her "slim waist." The brief depiction on the scene of her arrival the day before is praised as "the perfect lines" by Zhou Ji in the *Collections of Four Song Lyricists (Song Si Jia Ci Xuan)*. Readers may associate "a fairy amid clouds" with the immortal in Qu Yuan's *Songs of Chu (Chu Ci)*, the Wushan Goddess in Song Yu's *Ode to Gaotang (Gao Tang Fu)*, and the fantasy in Li

*A Picture of Ten Poems* by Zhang Xian

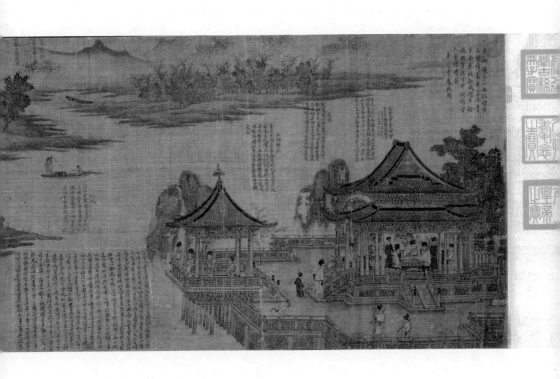

Bai's *A Dream Visit to the Tianmu Mountain*. Thus, the girl is visualized greatly by means of these traditional images.

The Tune *Whipping Dance in Intoxication*, as a rarely-seen tune, boasts noteworthy characteristics in rhyme and meter.

Next, let's come to another lyric by Zhang Xian.

**Tune: Buddhist Dancers**

*The zither grieves o'er Lady of River Xiang's death;*
*Green wave on wave exhales her everlasting breath.*
*Fine fingers touch the thirteen strings;*
*Slowly her heartfelt sorrow sings.*

*Her rippling eyes, feast to the sight;*
*Slanting jade pegs, wild geese in flight.*
*When her heart-breaking music thrills,*
*Her eyebrows lower like spring hills.*

The lyric vivifies a zither performance of a girl and describes her sorrow and hidden bitterness.

In the first stanza, "green wave on wave" represents the scenery and story about the Xiangjiang River. Then the lyric turns to the performer. "Fine fingers touch the thirteen strings" indicates the player is a young and charming girl and possibly a performer of the imperial music office. The Xiangjiang River is often connected with the sorrowful death of Lady of River Xiang who shed all her tears on the bamboos. "Slowly her heartfelt sorrow sings" conveys both the theme of the music itself and the fate of the performer and integrates them completely in this line.

The second stanza focuses more on the performer's expression. "Her rippling eyes, feast to the sight" depicts the girl's bright eyes, calm demeanor and the performance scenario. "Slanting jade pegs, wild geese in flight" describes the shape of the zither and echoes "strings" in the first stanza with "pegs." The pegs arranged in good order look like the flying wild geese. The lyricist also wrote "pegs and strings like formation of flying geese, giving sounds like springtime larks" in another renowned lyric *Song of Hawthorn*. At the end, the music is more and more sorrowful and the performer completely concentrates herself into the performance. Thus, the music is linked with the performer's heart and exhibits the girl's emotional world. From the lines "When her heart-breaking music thrills, Her eyebrows lower like spring hills," we even can imagine the tears in the performer's eyes. Critic Shen Jifei said, "the final lines are as perfect as the 'pegs and strings like formation of flying geese, giving sounds like springtime larks' in the *Song of Hawthorn*." Critic Huang Liaoyuan also praised the ending lines: "Are they about the zither music or the performer's thought or both? The sad and graceful sound expresses profound connotation and comforts the listeners and readers as well." These praises on the lines are both proper and correct.

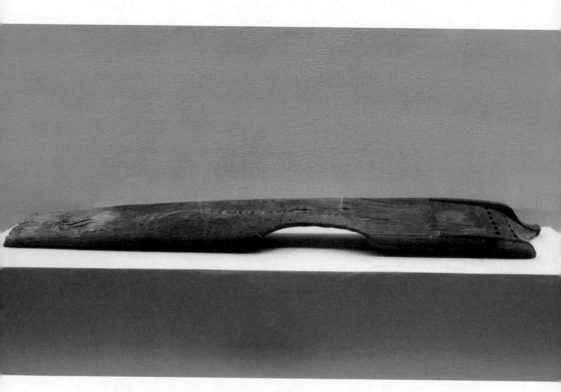

A 13-stringed Ancient Zither (Collected in Jiangxi Provincial Museum)

# Lovers Would Grieve at Parting as of Old
## – Appreciating the Bells Ringing in the Rain by Liu Yong

Yang Haiming

**Tune: Bells Ringing in the Rain**

*Cicadas chill*
*Drearily shrill.*
*We stand face to face in an evening hour*
*Before the pavilion, after a sudden shower.*
*Can we care for drinking before we part?*
*At the city gate*
*We are lingering late,*

*But the boat is waiting for me to depart.*
*Hand in hand we gaze at each other's tearful eyes*
*And burst into sobs with words congealed on our lips.*
*I'll go my way,*
*Far, far away.*
*On miles and miles of misty waves where sail ships,*
*And evening clouds hang low in boundless southern skies.*

*Lovers would grieve at parting as of old.*
*How could I stand this clear autumn day so cold!*
*Where shall I be found at daybreak*
*From wine awake?*
*Moored by a riverbank planted with willow trees*
*Beneath the waning moon and in the morning breeze.*
*I'll be gone for a year.*
*In vain would good times and fine scenes appear.*
*However gallant I am on my part,*
*To whom can I lay bare my heart?*

As the line "lovers would grieve at parting as of old" says, parting is a forever theme for writers.

Jiang Yan, a celebrity of the Southern Dynasties, was moved by the inevitable and pessimistic experience in life, and wrote the *Ode to the Parting*. After describing various partings, he sighed that even the most talented people couldn't clearly present the emotion at partings.

Indeed, humankind's emotions are surprisingly profound and complicated. The emotion at departure is the most difficult to describe. The mixed emotion on the gathering in the past and the separation in the future produces a pessimistic artistic aesthetism.

> *"Cut it, yet unsevered,*
> *Order it, the more tangled—*
> *Such is parting sorrow,*
> *Which dwells in my heart, too subtle a feeling to tell."*

The elusive taste of parting is the most difficult theme but also the theme most favored by numerous renowned writers for generations.

The Tang Dynasty, the golden days of lyric poetry, reached perfection in chanting the parting emotion. However, anyone that can depict new scenery and new emotion will create new realm and new representative pieces. So, the Song Dynasty also witnessed the production of masterpieces on parting. The *Bells Ringing in the Rain* by Liu Yong is an "ode to parting" of the Song Lyrics, marking the maturity of the Gracefulness School.

The *Bells Ringing in the Rain* delineates a parting by the ancient Bianhe River in the 11th century: On the outskirts of Bianliang (Today's Kaifeng, Henan province), the capital of the Northern Song Dynasty, a young couple are bidding farewell at a chilled dusk in autumn. Cicadas shrilling in willows, the outbound boat is waiting while the couple are gazing at each other and wouldn't separate for a

Liu Yong Memorial in Wuyi Mountain

single second. "It is only parting that makes people sad to the utmost." What a moving line it is!

In the lyric, different from historical legendary or politics-related departures, it is an ordinary parting, a dialogue between two common people, i.e., a frustrated talented scholar and a pretty and amorous girl. This indicates that love, a hidden and elusive topic in the previous eras, became an impressive theme in the Song Dynasty. With the rise of the citizen class in the Song Dynasty, the normal emotion between ordinary people and the universal humanity started to hold the spotlight of literature. On one hand, the accomplishments of lyricists are showed in the elaboration on ordinary people's passion and routine life instead of on exotic issues. On the other hand, the lyricist's expression is seasoned with the taste of humanity. With the gradual approaching to the late period of the fedual society, the humanity catering for the common people's aesthetics will surely win greater popularity among its appreciators. Now we analyze the lyric in details.

The parting was at a dusk in late autumn. What a sentimental timing it is! "Cicadas chill/Drearily shrill" indicates the depressive autumn and implies other verses lamenting over the arrival of autumn. Diction of good works can both ripple readers' emotion with scenic description as a medium and release the accumulated connotation in the words over a long period to awaken their personal experience and artistic association. The short line "Cicadas chill/Drearily shrill" sets the doleful keynote and dismal color of the entire parting scenario.

The parting location was the pavilion out of the city gate. Inside the city gate are busy streets and happy lovers. But the protagonist had to leave. "Pavilion" is a permanent image for departure in Chinese literature. Here, the symbolism and historical accumulation of the image jointly produce an unquenchable grief of parting.

Moreover, the parting is described in a slow tune, which further adds the anxiety of readers. In modern society, the departure is heart-broken, too, but only takes a few minutes. In the slow-paced middle ages, it often took several hours for a departure that consists of erecting a tent, having a farewell meal, drinking slowly and talking patiently... In the lyric, a sudden shower extended the departure. But, the short stay was like a bitter wine mixed with sweet. The longer the stay, the more bitter the departure would be. As expected, when the shower stopped, the boatman urged the protagonist to leave. Finally, the heart-broken departure moment came. The mood of parting reached the culmination. The lines "Hand in hand we gaze at each other's tearful eyes/And burst into sobs with words congealed on our lips" look like a close-up to completely present the scenario. The vague and implicit depiction on love by previous poets is totally abandoned here. The lyricist explicitly represented the silent heart-to-heart communication and dialogue between the couple and

A Lady Misses People Faraway against a Willow, from *Pictures on Characters and Landscape* by You Qiu of the Ming Dynasty

vivified their moving expressions and emotion in the verse based on his own travel and departure experiences. Love is a theme often neglected or ignored in orthodox literature in the feudal times. But, Liu Yong elaborated it to the utmost as an eye-catching topic. Actually, it is a shift of literature vogue. So, in the lyric, instead of implicitness, connotation and tenderness, Liu applied a style featuring explicitness, openness and directness. To sum up, the first stanza starts from the gloomy "Cicadas chill/Drearily shrill" to the depressive "Hand in hand we gaze at each other's tearful eyes/And burst into sobs with words congealed on our lips," and then switches to the unrestricted lines "I'll go my way,/ Far, far away./On miles and miles of misty waves where sail ships,/And evening clouds hang low in boundless southern skies" at the end of the stanza. Once the restrained emotion is released, it overflows like water from a dyke breach. "The structure of the stanza seems like a dragon trapped in a shallow pond finally takes off and dances in the sky," said Tang Guizhang in *A Brief Explanation to Tang and Song's Lyrics (Tang Song Ci Jian Shi)*.

"Lovers would grieve at parting as of old./How could I stand this clear autumn day so cold" initiates the second stanza with the grievous parting and chilly autumn to highlight the dual pessimism. However, the most excellent and elegant lines in the lyric come: "Where shall I be found at daybreak/From wine awake? /Moored by a riverbank planted with willow trees/Beneath the waning moon and in the morning breeze." The lines not only combine the scenery and the emotion but also render the emotion from an ordinary parting scene. Relying on the special rhyme and meter of the tune, Liu Yong created a novel, exquisite and elegant artistic world. These lines have been passed on for generation after generation.

First, the verses depict the natural and "true scenery," the dancing willows by the bank of the Bianhe River. When waking up the next morning inside the floating boat from the hangover, the protagonist was already far away from his lover. "Moored by a riverbank planted with willow trees/Beneath the waning moon and in the morning breeze" completely delineate the scenery seen from the floating boat.

Second, the lines represent the "true emotion." "Moored by a riverbank planted with willow trees/Beneath the waning moon and in the morning breeze" are not only a simple description of scenery but also an impressive expression of emotion which can be seen from the images. In the verses "A row of willows shades the riverside. / Their long, long swaying twigs have dyed/The mist in green./How many times has the ancient Dyke seen/The lovers part while wafting willow down/And drooping twigs caress the stream along the town!" by Zhou Bangyan (Sovereign of Wine), willow is both the image for and the witness of parting. Seeing the willows on a floating boat alone, the protagonist couldn't help missing his girl.

25

The ancient  Bianhe River in the *Along the River During the Qingming Festival* (Part) by Zhang Zeduan of the Song Dynasty

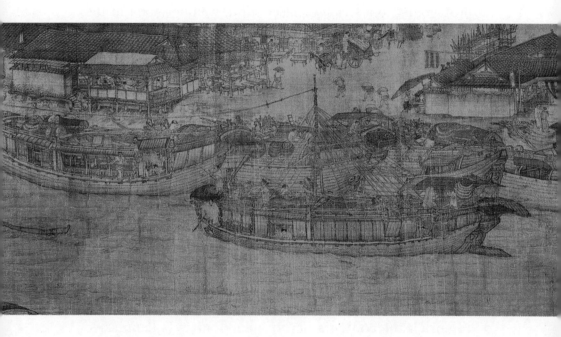

"Beneath the waning moon and in the morning breeze" describes a further feeling of the lonely traveler. Just imagine: on the previous day, the couple were drinking together and gazing at each other hand in hand, but, now, a sudden breeze drove away the tipsy feeling and pushed the protagonist to a strange place with a waning moon in the sky. The inner agony became extremely severe. Only those with similar experience will have the real psychological feeling. So, the verses describe the "true emotion."

Third, based on the "true scenery" and "true emotion," the lyricist created a gentle and graceful new conception, i.e. the special style combining extreme dismay and beauty. Ordinary writers often can feel the dismay of parting deeply, only outstanding ones can also represent the beauty of parting. The lines delineate a picture: Withered willows waft by the riverside in the autumn wind; the lovesick traveler watch the waning moon alone. Not only the loneliness but also the tragic color are highlighted to enrich the contents of lyric and convey a depressive love and a vague beauty. It is the typical style of the Gracefulness School. No wonder the later scholars regard these lines as the representative of Liu Yong and event the Gracefulness School's lyrics.

Thus, the lyric develops to a profound and connotative realm. But, then, it comes back to the parting. Actually, the lines "Moored by a riverbank planted with willow trees/ Beneath the waning moon and in the morning breeze" is

*Withered Willows in a Riverside Village* by Gong Xian of the Qing Dynasty

The Grand Canal of China in the *Picture on the Southern Inspection of Emperor Kangxi* (Part) by Wang Hui of the Qing Dynasty

just imagination for the next day's journey. The skill of depicting "real emotion" with "imaginative expression" enriches the lyric's profoundness. Next come the lines "I'll be gone for a year./In vain would good times and fine scenes appear./However gallant I am on my part,/To whom can I lay bare my heart?" which outline the realistic love and the special mood of the girl. Frankly, these lines are too "open." But, in term of style, the lyric starts in a restricted way but ends in a quite open expression. The variation of style makes readers ignore the "flaw." Instead, readers can feel the ingeniousness of "the skillful expression of the complete emotion."

In one word, the lyric elaborates the heart-broken parting of a loving couple, praises the ideal of a secular and somewhat seclusive living, and expresses a new psychology at that time to a certain degree. Artistically speaking, the lyric makes full use of the advantages of the slow tune in describing human's emotion complexity with its detailed narration and skillful combination.

"In the morning breeze under the waning moon, how can I forget the lyricist Liu Yong?" The lines by Wang Shizhen of the Qing Dynasty described the later generations' adoration to this famous lyric and its writer. In the *Romance of the Western Chamber* (Parting at Pavilion), a noted opera of the Yuan Dynasty, we can see the influence of this lyric.

Great Leisure in a Small Bower
– Appreciation of Yan Shu's Silk-washing Stream

Zhong Ling

## Tune: Silk-washing Stream

*By double-curtained bower I see swallows pass;*
*Red petals of late flowers fall on green grass,*
*The winding rails' shadow mingles with ripples cold.*

*A sudden gale blows and ruffles emerald screen.*
*How many times has rain dripped on lotus leaves green?*
*Awake from wine, the grief to see guests gone makes*
*me old.*

Yan Shu was renowned for depicting leisure time and elegant life. The lyric quoted above is one of Yan's masterpieces.

According to the Western Garden entry in the Chenzhou section of the *Chorography of Henan (He Nan Tong Zhi)* compiled by Wang Shijun of the Qing Dynasty, the Western Garden was situated at the west of the Chenzhou township, and built by Zhang Yong, the magistrate in the Song Dynasty. Western Garden consisted of seven pavilions, i.e. Liufang, Zhongyan, Liubei, Xiangyin, Huancui, Xixin and Wangjing, a chamber named Yinfeng, a hall called Qingsi and a platform Wanghu. Yan Shu lived in the garden as a retired prime minister of the Song Court. According to Yan's description in *Grass in the Courtyard (Ting Sha Ji),* on the ground between the Qingsi Hall and the Zhongyan Pavilion, the grass was growing prosperously due to rare disturbance of people. Yan asked his servants to transplant the grass and build a grassland, thus a tranquil and exquisite garden was set up. Yan lived a joyful life in the breezy and tidy place. The lyric was composed in the late spring of the Eighth Year of the Qingli Period under the reign of Emperor Renzong of the Song Dynasty (1048). In the spring of that year, Yan was transferred from Yingzhou to Chenzhou as a magistrate.

The first stanza describes the views seen in leisure. The "double-curtained bower" highlights the leisure of the residence through the depiction of the tranquil and seclusive environment. The line "I see swallows pass" indicates the lyricist realized the swallows and the micro changes in the courtyard at the leisure time while he neglected the natural beauties in those busy and noisy days. The famous lines "Swallows that skimmed by painted eaves in bygone days, are dipping now among the humble homes' doorways" in the *Black Robe Lane* by Liu Yuxi apply the same image to sigh for the vicissitudes. Likewise, the "swallows" in this lyric turbine disturb the tranquility, implying the agitation of the lyricist's mood and ushering in the picturesque frames. The line "Red petals of late flowers fall on green grass" makes a sharp contrast between the fading red and the flourishing green, displaying the splendor of the late spring. "The winding rails' shadow mingles with ripples cold" describes the desolation after the banquet and suggests the approaching of dusk with the "winding rails' shadow."

The Portrait of Yan Shu

*Bird and Flowers* by Zhou Zhimian of the Ming Dynasty

The "passing swallows," "falling flowers" and "rippling shadow" are not only the presentation of the desolation after a banquet but also the changes of the lyricist's view angles from inside to outside, up to low, and from air to water. More importantly, they are the reflection of the volatile inner feelings of the lyricist. What a leisure mood the lyricist had to gaze at these subtle changes and changing images! In addition, the gradual deceleration of the actions of these images shows the lyricist's mind toward slightness, subtleness and profoundness.

The second stanza depicts the sound and meditation in the leisure. "A sudden gale blows and ruffles emerald screen." The breeze brings coolness slightly, silently and elusively to the bower. "How many times has rain dripped on lotus leaves green? I listen to the patter of rain on the withered lotus" by Li Shangyin describes the lotus in autumn rain. But Yan's line is on the green lotus in late spring, while Li's verse on the withered lotus in late autumn. "For many times" indicates the tranquil environment and the author's leisure mood.

The ending "awake from wine, the grief to see guests gone makes me old" clarifies the theme. "Awake from wine to see guests gone" indicates the previous five lines exhibit the tranquility and leisure after the banquet. Describing tranquility may often be difficult with still life, but may be easy with dynamic ones. Against the backdrop with the "passing swallows", "falling flowers," "rippling

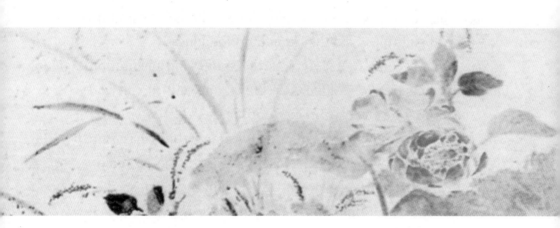

*Lotus* (Part) by Wang Wen of the Ming Dynasty

shadow" and "the drizzle" are the calm and steady eyes of the lyricist who was concentrating on appreciating the scenery. "The grief to see guests gone makes me old" suggests the lyricist's sorrow and depression behind the colorful delineation of the place. In particular, "red petals of late flowers fall on green grass" is the most impressive line, which contrasts the red fallen petals with the green flourishing grass, implies the philosophy of existence and extinction and is associated with the vicissitudes of the world. Yan Shu was deprived from the prime minister office in 1044 and had been apart from the capital for four years when composing the lyric. So, readers often can feel a slight sadness from Yan's leisure and graceful lines.

Yan Shu had lived a rich and smooth life in the peaceful period under the reign of Emperor Zhenzong and Emperor Renzong of the Song Dynasty. He was satisfactory with the stable and tranquil environment. He believed in the universe was filled and pervaded with various resources and emotions which were harmoniously coexisting. Thus, the leisure and the exquisite feeling dominates his works. However, the court struggles, the political conflicts and the fluctuation in his career produced profound influence to his lyrics. Therefore, a sentimental atmosphere is often found in his leisure-theme works.

# A Different Understanding to Yan Jidao's Renowned Couplet

Zang Kejia

### Tune: Partridge in Sky

*Time and again with rainbow sleeves you tried to fill*
*My cup with wine that, drunk, I kept on drinking still.*
*You danced till the moon hung low over the willow trees;*
*You sang until amid peach blossoms blushed the breeze.*
*Then came the time to part,*
*But you're deep in my heart.*
*How many times have I met you in dreams at night!*
*Now left to gaze at you in silver candlelight,*

41

*I fear it is not you,*
*But a sweet dream untrue.*

Yan Jidao was a famous lyricist of the Song Dynasty with many lyrics passed on for generations. His most outstanding work is the *Tune: Partridge in Sky* (Time and again with rainbow sleeves you tried to fill). The lyric is known for its bold description of love and moving description of psychology. Its exquisite diction and sonorous melody have kept on moving its readers. "You danced till the moon hung low over the willow trees; You sang until amid peach blossoms blushed the breeze," a

Photocopy of *Collections of Yan Jidao's Lyrics (Xiao Shan Ci)*

noted couplet in the renowned lyric, ushers the readers into a poetic and picturesque courtyard. The singing and dancing of the heroine is filled with enthusiastic romance. The hero, even without wine, is intoxicated by her charming demeanor and her fair-sounding voice. All hearts are connected, and all people share the same feeling. So, all lovers in the world can experience the love between the couple in the lyric.

Reciting the couplet, one can't help being intoxicated by the flamboyant atmosphere. The couplet brings lively visual and sound aestheticism, but it is also elusive for readers to appreciate. Readers can intuitively feel its wonderfulness but they cannot clearly define what the wonderfulness is.

I have read several different understandings on the couplet. Most are literal and far-fetched explanations or eisegesis. After emotionally chanting the couplet alone for many times and pondering on the diction again and again, I have explored a unique field to enjoy the lines. Maybe my understanding doesn't meet the real scenario. However, it is my idiographic findings.

In my opinion, the dancing and signing described in the lyric was in a courtyard instead of in a chamber. Yan Jidao, son of the prime minister for Emperor Renzong of the Song Dynasty, had a courtyard dotted with pavilions and platforms for leisure and recreation. After some drink, he and the girl pleasantly came to the courtyard planted

*Willows and Peach Blossoms in Spring* by Wang Wu of the Qing Dynasty

with willows and peach trees. The girl kept on dancing joyfully till the moon hung low over the willow trees. She was so excited. Then, with a decorated fan in her hand, she sung her love out aloud amid the blooming peach trees. According to this assumption, the romantic and picturesque delineation meets the lovers' feeling in a more appropriate way.

Lyrics have no fixed and definite explanation. Readers can have various understandings and opinions to the same work based on their own mood, appreciation accomplishments and aesthetic abilities. There is no standard answer in lyric appreciation. Even the author himself could not give a fairly clear explanation to his work. My understanding above mentioned is based on my prudent consideration over a long period.

# Sighs of a Heartbroken Lyricist
## – On *Riverside Daffodils* by Yan Jidao

Huang Ke

## Tune: Riverside Daffodils

*Awake from dreams, I find the locked tower high;*
*Sober from wine, I see the curtain hanging low.*
*As last year spring grief seems to grow.*
*Amid the falling blooms alone stand I;*
*In the fine rain a pair of swallows fly.*

*I still remember when I first saw pretty Ping,*
*In silken dress embroidered with two hearts in a ring,*

*Revealing lovesickness by touching pipa's string.*
*The moon shines bright just as last year;*
*It did see her like a cloud disappear.*

In early Song Dynasty, the lyricists continued the tradition of the Southern Tang, graceful in style but narrow and inanimate in theme. Due to the pervasive bias that lyrics were subordinate to poems and only expressions of amorousness, poems and essays were the classical means for majestic themes while lyrics had been continuing its traditional themes on charming love. During this period, the recognized lyricist who had been apt in the sector with ease and established a writing style comparable to the Southern Tang's last emperor and lyricist Li Yu was Yan Jidao, also known as the Junior Yan.

Yan Jidao was the youngest son of Yan Shu, the Senior Yan, who was the prime minister of Emperor Renzhong of the Song Dynasty and lived a noble and rich life. Yan Shu, boasting a noble, fresh and gorgeous style in lyrics, was actually a leader of lyricists in early Song Dynasty. Yan Jidao, born with a silver spoon in his mouth, had been well edified and thus obtained profound artistic accomplishments. But, he was too naive to adapt to the sophisticated society. His contemporary Huang Tingjian said the Junior Yan was utterly ignorant to the the way of the world in the Preface to *Collections of Yan Jidao's Lyrics (Xiao Shan Ci)*. Thus, the unsophisticated Junior Yan

Photocopy of *Supplement to Lyrics (Yue Fu Bu Wang)*

had only got a low-rank post in Xutian Town, Yingchang Prefecture (Today's Xuchang, Henan province) and couldn't make a basic living. Similar with the experience of the Southern Tang's last emperor and lyricist Li Yu, the Junior Yan also experienced both the noble life and the embarrassing situation, and shared a common mood with the depressed emperor. Because of this, Feng Menghua, a critic of the Qing Dynasty, said that the Junior Yan was a "heartbroken lyricist in ancient times."

According to the *Anthology of 61 Lyricists of the Song Dynasty*, Feng Menghua said that "Qin Guan and Yan Jidao were both heartbroken lyricists in ancient times." However, in *Jen-Chien Tz'u-hua (Opinions on Traditional Lyrics)*, Wang Guowei said that "Yan Jidao was less competitive to Qin Guan in expressing great connotation and significance with flat diction due to Yan's excessively noble style." But I don't agree with Wang at this point. Yan's nobleness in his works is mainly the reminiscences of the elapsed glories and beauties which were like the moon in the water and flowers in the mirror. For instance, in *Butterflies in Love with Flowers*, he once made a deep sigh "How easily the gathering and separation take place! It is loneliness that accompanies me always!" based on his own heartbroken experience from nobleness to poorness, from joyfulness to depression. Moreover, Yan was also a skillful lyricist in "expressing great connotation and significance with flat diction." I would like to prove this with his *Riverside Daffodils*.

Lovesickness at a Moonlit Night from the *Pictures of Beauties* by Fei Danyu of the Qing Dynasty

The lyric is about the singer Ping, one of the four female singers served at the homes of Shen Lianshu and Chen Junchong who were friends of Yan Jidao. Yan, Shen and Chen often held parties and composed lyrics for the girls to sing. Later on, Shen was ill and Chen died. The four girls were also scattered, and Yan lost contact with them. This lyric is Yan's sigh for the elapse of the happy time and the dreamlike bygones.

The starting lines "Awake from dreams, I find the locked tower high; Sober from wine, I see the curtain hanging low" describe the lyricist had to face the cruel reality and agony after a temporary evasion. In a dream, the lyricist enjoyed a banquet in the tower and a performance on the curtained stage. But, the lyricist fell into the loneliness in reality again after awaking.

In the shadow of loneliness, "spring grief", an elusive dismay, bites the lyricist's heart. "As last year spring grief seems to grow. Amid the falling blooms alone stand I; In the fine rain a pair of swallows fly." Watching at the falling pedals and a pair of willows flying in the drizzle, the lonely lyricist stood in the courtyard silently, unaware of pedals falling on his shoulders. "The lonely I" and "the pair of swallows" constitute a sharp contrast, arousing the lyricist's sentimental mood. Thus, the lyric naturally turns to the second stanza and switches to the beautiful memory on Ping.

The couplet "Amid the falling blooms alone stand I; In the fine rain a pair of swallows fly" has been highly praised for its high diction technique and profound connotation. However, the lyricist directly borrowed the couplet from *Late Spring by* Weng Hong, a poet lived in period between Tang and Song dynasties. The couplet vivified the "state without consciousness" defined in *Jen-Chien Tz'u-hua* and the depression, loneliness and nostalgia of the lyricist in the realistic world.

Finally, the second stanza ushers in Ping, the reason for spring grief, in the first line "I still remember when I first saw pretty Ping." Ping was one of the said four songstresses and favored by the lyricist. According to Yan's description in other lyrics, Ping was a naive, graceful and beautiful girl. The first impression often initiated an affair and had epoch-making significance. It was the source of the lyricist's joy and sadness and frequently came to the lyricist's mind. So, the lyricist represented his "first sight" at Ping to showcase her beauty and his love to her.

Ping was "in silken dress embroidered with two hearts in a ring" when the lyricist first saw her. She was in fashionable and graceful attire and quite different from the tawdry songstresses. The "embroidery with two hearts in a ring" indicates the girl's uniqueness in ornaments, and hints her first awakening of love and cherishing fond dreams of love. The line suggested they fell in love at the first sight and expected their future romance.

Next, "Revealing lovesickness by touching pipa's string" praised Ping's high skill in playing the instrument.

More important, the lyricist could enjoy and understand Ping's music. Their emotional exchanges were further strengthened through her devoted performance and the lyricist's devoted enjoyment.

At the end, the lyricist didn't describe their ogle exchanges or honeyed words. Instead, he wrote the farewell: "The moon shines bright just as last year; It did see her like a cloud disappear." Bathed in the bright moonshine, Ping vanished like a colorful cloud. According to the description, Ping transformed from a fashionable girl, to a sweetheart playing pipa and then to a flying fairy, suggesting the gradual intensification, purification and ascension of the love between the lyricist and Ping. Now, Ping is the embodiment of beauty, and the lyricist seems to meet her in a fairy land. No doubt, it is a high-profile presentation of beauty to the lyricist and the readers as well.

However, all the good bygones cannot be recovered. The lyricist was entangled in the past good time and could not come out, which intensified his distress. The distress was expressed in a connotative way with the verse "the moon shines bright just as last year" which contains meanings in two tiers: on one hand, it indicates that Ping was especially brilliant on the departure day when a bright moon hung on the sky; on the other hand, the moon is still on the sky tonight, but I don't know where to find Ping. Thus, the lyricist's lovesickness, the source of his spring grief, was completely unveiled. The lyricist felt depressed and sentimental at the past good days and the disappeared beauty, and composed the nostalgic lyrics with a broken heart.

# "It Is not the Singer's Pain I Pity, but Few Are Those Who Understand the Song!"
## — Appreciating Yan Jidao's *Riverside Daffodils* from a Broader Aspect

Miao Yue

The *Riverside Daffodils* (Awake from dreams, I find the locked tower high) by Northern Song's Yan Jidao, a popular masterpiece through the ages, has been highly praised by critics and collected in renowned lyric anthologies. Critic Yu Pingbo also collected and elaborated the lyric in his Explanation *of Selected Tang and Song's Lyrics (Tang Song Ci Xuan Shi)*, contributing a lot to reader's comprehension to the work. In this paper, I attempt to express my appreciation and association from a more profound aspect.

Yan Jidao, alias Shuyuan, was a special one in disposition, temperament and personality amid conventional Chinese scholars. As the seventh son of Yan Shu, the prime minister and literature master in the Northern Song, he had been dedicated to studying the classical six arts and various schools of thinkers and achieving fairly profound cultural accomplishments. Based on his family status and accomplishments, he would easily climb up the social ladder. But, being indifferent to fame and benefit, he neither attended the imperial examinations nor served the noble families. Ancient scholars pursued official positions for realizing personal political ambitions or family honor and economic benefits. Yan, believing himself incapable in governmental management, had no interest in high ranks and benefits. As a son of the prime minister, he had witnessed severe struggle between cliques and detested the officialdom. Despite of his scorn to officialdom, he had taken some low-rank offices in Xutian Town and Kaifeng thanks to his family status, and then quit to his residence in the capital (Bianliang, today's Kaifeng in Henan province) and lived a secluded life there.

Similar with his uniqueness in officialdom, Yan was also a lonely lyricist in literati. Generally speaking, Yan Jidao, a talented youth with an influential father in literati, could easily establish his name in the circles. But Yan had seldom contact with his contemporary scholars except

*A Beauty Plays the Pipa* by Wu Wei of the
Ming Dynasty

Huang Tingjian, a famous scholar with special opinions on literature and arts. In his *Preface to Collections of Yan Jidao's Lyrics (Xiao Shan Ci Xu)*, Huang praised that Yan's works "feature a mighty and moving force due to his application of poetic diction in lyrics." Also, the preface highlighted Yan's naiveness, uprightness, unsophistication and ingenuousness in the worldly society.

Except Huang Tingjian, other renowned scholars, such as Su Shi, Su Zhe, Qin Guan, Cao Buzhi, Zhang Lei and Chen Shidao, had no communications with Yan Jidao. Yan's uprightness was rather excessive sometimes. Once, Su Shi, then the member of the Imperial Academy, intended to visit him for his reputation in lyrics and Huang's recommendation. But Yan refused Su possibly because of the visitor's high position in officialdom. Actually, Su Shi, a capable and farsighted genius, should be the one that could appreciate Yan's sentiment and ability. Unfortunately, Yan gave up the opportunity.

As above mentioned, Yan Jidao was lonesome in both officialdom and literati. However, he couldn't live a rustic life like Tao Yuanming did in the Jin Dynasty. He had to live in the prosperous Bianliang. Where could he find a tranquil place to evade from the worldly uproar? Finally he made friends with Shen Lianshu and Chen Junlong who were wealthy and had no interest in officialdom. Shen and Chen had several songstresses, namely, Lian, Hong, Ping and Yun. So, Yan, Shen and Chen often drank together

The Maid Qingwen from *Illustrations to A Dream of Red Mansions* by Gai Qi of the Qing Dynasty

and enjoyed the girls' performance. The girls were naive, honest, talented and versatile, and favored by Yan who wrote lyrics for them to play. Ping was Yan's favorite girl. The *Riverside Daffodils* to be commented below was about Yan's reminiscences of Ping.

> *Awake from dreams, I find the locked tower high;*
> *Sober from wine, I see the curtain hanging low.*
> *As last year spring grief seems to grow.*
> *Amid the falling blooms alone stand I;*
> *In the fine rain a pair of swallows fly.*
> *I still remember when I first saw pretty Ping,*
> *In silken dress embroidered with two hearts in a ring,*
> *Revealing lovesickness by touching pipa's string.*
> *The moon shines bright just as last year;*
> *It did see her like a cloud disappear.*

It is a lyric composed with fairly high rhetorical skills, such as couplet, repetition and contrast. The initial couplet is about the loneliness of the lyricist. The place where the lyricist and Ping enjoyed drinking and singing was deserted after a hangover. Then, the lyric comes to the reminiscences in two sections. "As last year spring grief seems to grow. Amid the falling blooms alone stand I; In the fine rain a pair of swallows fly" describe a closer memory while the other lines depict a further memory. Although these are memories, the descriptions on images are vivid, beautiful and realistic,

*Peach Blossoms, Willows and Swallows*
by Liu Yanchong of the Qing Dynasty

intensifying the lyricist's loneliness and unforgettable love to Ping. "Amid the falling blooms alone stand I; In the fine rain a pair of swallows fly" is a couplet directly borrowed from a poem by Weng Hong, a poet lived in period between Tang and Song dynasties. The images here are extremely beautiful and appropriate in the lyric. In the second stanza, the beauty and talent of Ping was not directly presented. Instead, Ping's beauty was highlighted by her costume—"in silken dress embroidered with two hearts in a ring", Ping's talent by her skill—"revealing lovesickness by touching pipa's string." The ending couplet expresses the lyricist's great yearning for Ping and deep disappointment in a connotative way: Ping was like a cloud in moonshine; however, the moon shines still while Ping had vanished. The application of a series of dazzling images, such as tower, curtain, falling blooms, fine rain, silken dress, pipa, moon and cloud, builds a fairy place for Ping to live in.

However, was Ping really such a lofty girl as Yan's description? Could Ping understand the connotation and realm in the lyric?

To the first question, in my opinion, Yan idealized the image of Ping just like Jia Baoyu's idealization of Qingwen in the elegy *Ode to Lotus described in A Dream of Red Mansions.*

And the second question is worthy of discussion. Throughout the past 2,000 years, Chinese scholars have cherished two complexes: promoting the morals, pursuing the knowledge. Ever since the Spring and Autumn and the Warring States periods, Chinese scholars have been trying to assist the monarch's governance through promoting morals. Occasionally they achieved in the Warring States Period, but since then scholars had often been prosecuted or even executed by the governors. As for pursuing knowledge, it is also rather difficult to meet a bosom friend sharing common understandings in thoughts, morals, study and arts. So, the mutual understanding between Zhuang Zhou and Huishi in philosophy, and between Boya and Ziqi in zither art, has been praised for hundreds of years. While Yang Xiong's expectation on being understood by later generations was deemed a tragedy. As for Yan Jidao, he probably had no complex to serve the monarch and promote morals. So, "pursuing the knowledge" should be a necessary complex for him. Huang Tingjin was the only scholar that appreciated Yan's talents in literati. Yan surely expected someone else to enjoy his talents. But Ping and other songstresses couldn't understand Yan's innermost as they were lack of high cultural accomplishments. Even if Ping read the *Riverside Daffodils*, she might not enjoy Yan's supreme creation skills and the profound connotation contained in the work.

In the *Northwest the Tall Tower Stands* of *the 19 Poems of Eastern Han Dynasty* there are lines "It is not the singer's pain I pity, but few are those who understand the song!" Actually, this has been a constant pity since ancient times.

# On *Beautiful Lady Yu* by Yan Jidao

Zhang Ming

## Tune: Beautiful Lady Yu

*Enjoying the Golden Dress Tune in a moonlit plum garden,*
*I remember the days with my talented girl friend.*
*Why has the romance gone away with spring wind?*
*All leaves become green overnight,*
*To replace the fallen pedals flying overhead.*

*Lotus sweetly blooms;*
*Oaring quickly, approaching are the good days.*

63

*Will you come when lotus matures?*
*Upon intoxicated me, flowers cast their shadows;*
*Then, who will support me and set my heart at ease?!*

It might not be the supreme work of Yan Jidao's lyrics. It seems that the lyric is shallow in expression and simple in diction at the first sight. However, anyone who reads it with great concentration will have a deep impression to the elegance described in the ending lines "Upon intoxicated me, flowers cast their shadows; Who will support me and set my heart at ease?!" Moreover, once understanding the final lines, you will have a better appreciation to the previous lines and comprehend the underlying delight of the seemingly plain description. Actually, the impressive ending is painstakingly elaborated by the lyricist and worthy of a profound study.

Most of Yan's love lyrics were composed for a definite person, a songstress or a beloved girl. The initial two lines indicate that this lyric was written for a songstress who was talented, clever and competent comparable to the renowned Zhuo Wenjun of the Han Dynasty. The scene "a moonlit plum garden" highlights both the elegance of the environment and the gracefulness of the girl. It must be an impressive scene deeply rooted in Yan's brain. The linkage between the character and scene at the beginning offers a concrete association image for the romance. Structurally speaking, the scene is also echoed by the "upon intoxicated

Lady Zhuo Wenjun of *Renowned Beauties in History*
by Lu Chang of the Qing Dynasty

me, flowers cast their shadows" at the end. Moreover, the seemingly intemperate conduct described at the ending lines is attached with complicated but definite sentimental meanings thanks to the initial scene description.

The second stanza vivifies the hesitation, the lovesickness and the expectation. "Oaring quickly, approaching are the good days" are lines skillfully converted from ancient verses by Yan to visualize the eagerness and expectation. Next comes the question "will you come when lotus matures," both releasing the eagerness and intensifying the yearning of the lyricist through the artful structuring. Naturally, the ending scene of intoxication deeply impresses the readers. Here, the lines "upon intoxicated me, flowers cast their shadows; Then, who will support me and set my heart at ease" were rewritten by Yan based on verses of Tang's poet Lu Guimeng to express an emotion completely different from Lu's intemperateness.

Here is the *Awakening in a Spring Evening* by Lu Guimeng for our further comparison.

> *Having roamed about for years,*
> *Once drunk,*
> *Collapsing in a wineshop sometimes;*
> *Awakening to find the moon rises,*
> *Upon conscious me, flowers cast their shadows;*
> *Then, who will support me and set my heart at ease?*

First, Yan's lyric, written for his sweetheart, expresses the eagerness and the expectation for the date. While Lu's poem, written for his friend, described a hangover experience. Lu's description is about the life of an unrestrained and intemperate hermit and quite different from that of Yan in both content and style.

Second, Yan's lyric has a wide span of time and space as well as a comprehensive psychological description. Lu's poem is just about a hangover, short in time, simple in content and plain in psychology.

Third, Yan's emotional description is intensive and persistent, such as the complaint about "why has the romance gone away with spring wind," the exaggeration of "all leaves become green overnight, To replace the fallen pedals flying overhead" and the expectation of "Will you come when lotus matures." So, the final lines express the intense mood with the drunkenness. However, Lu's poem is much more vivacious and relaxed than that of Yan in expression and diction.

Fourth, Yan's lyric and Lu's poem are different in structural and linguistic characteristics. Lu's poem features straightforward structure: a drunken experience in his profligate and immoderate routine life. But Yan's lyric is complicated and discrete in structure, starting from "enjoying music in a moonlit plum garden" to "memories on the old days, the departure, the yearning for reunion" and the lyricist's lovesick psychology and acts.

Fifth, Yan's ending lines "upon intoxicated me, flowers

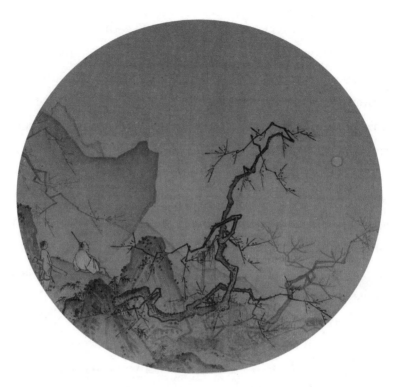

*Enjoying Wintersweet at a Moonlit Night* by Ma Yuan of the Song Dynasty

cast their shadows; Then, who will support me and set my heart at ease" echo the initial "enjoying the Golden Dress Tune in a moonlit plum garden" in images and connotative meanings to highlight the lyricist's deep love to the songstress. On the contrast, Lu's poem is not as complicated as Yan's work in context.

The aforesaid contrast shows that Yan's work is different from Lu's in context, mood, situation, rhythm, cadence and especially in expression. Also, Yan's diction change from "conscious" to "intoxicated" is richer in artistic connotation and expression than Lu's original version. Yan's change in context and rhetoric produces a completely different style and effect.

Therefore, from this lyric of Yan, we can know that the connotation and expression of diction are determined by not only diction itself but also the restriction of context. So, it is not enough to evaluate a work only based on its words and sentences.

# The Masterpiece of a "Veteran Fox"
– Appreciating Wang Anshi's *Fragrance of Laurel Branch: In Memory of the Ancient Capital*

Zhang Bowei

## Tune: Fragrance of Laurel Branch

*In Memory of the Ancient Capital*

*I climb the height*
*And stretch my sight:*
*Late autumn just begins its gloomy time.*
*The ancient capital looks sublime.*
*The limpid river, beltlike, flows a thousand miles;*
*Emerald peaks on peaks tower in piles.*

The Masterpiece of a "Veteran Fox"
– Appreciating Wang Anshi's Fragrance of Laurel
Branch: In Memory of the Ancient Capital

In the declining sun sails come and go;
Against west wind wineshop streamers flutter high and
low.
The painted boat
In cloud afloat,
Like stars in Silver River egrets fly.
What a picture before the eye!

The days gone by
Saw people in opulence vie.
Alas! Shame on shame came under the walls,
In palace halls.
Leaning on rails, in vain I utter sighs
Over ancient kingdoms' fall and rise.
The running water saw the Six Dynasties pass,
But I see only chilly mist and withered grass.
Even now and again
The songstresses still sing
The song composed in vain
By a captive king.

*Fragrance of Laurel Branch: In Memory of the Ancient Capital* is a famous work written by Wang Anshi in Jinling (Today's Nanjing, Jiangsu province).

Among the 30-odd lyrics on Jinling composed simultaneously by his contemporary noted lyricists, Wang Anshi's work is the uncontroversial No. 1. "Wang is really like a veteran fox," Su Shi praised him sincerely, with great admiration to Wang's talents showed in this lyric. It is well known that Wang was equally matched with Su in essays and poems, but less competent in lyrics. But, when this one appeared, Su showed great respect to Wang's talent in lyrics. So, let's find out the reason for that.

The lyric consists of two stanzas: the first one on the scenery of Jinling, and the second on the memories of and emotion to the ancient capital.

Jinling, the capital for six historical dynasties, had been a prosperous place in southern China. Autumn, as a bleak and chilly season, has been arousing sighs of scholars since ancient times in China. In the lyric, Wang started the first stanza with "I climb the height/And stretch my sight:/Late autumn just begins its gloomy time. /The ancient capital looks sublime" to indicate the time, place and his mood in the season. Next come "the limpid river, beltlike, flows a thousand miles" to describe the majesty of the Yangtze River, and "emerald peaks on peaks tower in piles" to delineate the static distant scenery. Then the lines "in the declining sun sails come and go; against west wind wineshop streamers flutter high and low" depict the dynamic nearby views. On the Qinhuai River there were painted boats, hustling and bustling at a dazzling night. The brilliant colors, the flying birds and the floating clouds are vivified in lines "the painted boat/In cloud afloat, / Like stars in Silver River egrets fly. /What a picture before the eye!" All these are views from "I climb the height/And

72

*The Masterpiece of a "Veteran Fox"*
*– Appreciating Wang Anshi's Fragrance of Laurel*
*Branch: In Memory of the Ancient Capital*

stretch my sight." The "declining sun" and "west wind" usher in the sighs in the second stanza.

At the prosperous view, the lyricist recalled "people in opulence vie" in the past days. Relying on the affluence of southern China, the rulers of the Southern Dynasties had lived a life of wanton extravagance, resulting their successive decadence and perdition, which is summarized in the lines "Alas! Shame on shame came under the walls, in palace halls.Leaning on rails, in vain I utter sighs/Over ancient kingdoms' fall and rise." Recalling the historical ups and downs, successes and failures, Wang Anshi hoped to make reform based on historical lessons. He knew that any sigh or meditation would be useless if no reform and improvement were made. This is the difference between Wang and ordinary scholars. Wang's outstanding views,

*Clearing Autumn Skies over Mountains and Valleys* (Part)

novel and profound conception are the keys to highlight the lyric's position amid the works in the period.

However, lyrics are not the best literature type for argumentation. So, the lyricist came back to depiction: "The running water saw the Six Dynasties pass, But I see only chilly mist and withered grass." All historical figures and events have gone by, only chilly mist and withered grass make no change. Here the withered grass, a frequent image for "sadness" in poems and lyrics, symbolizes the deep sorrow in Wang's innermost. Finally, the lyric ends with "Even now and again/The songstresses still sing/The song composed in vain/By a captive king." The lines are Wang's paraphrase of the verses by poet Du Mu. Moreover, based on Du Mu's lines, Wang creatively applied the impressive adverbial modifiers like "even now and again" and "still" to produce a shocking effect. In general, Wang Anshi was not comparable with Su Shi in composing lyrics. But this lyric won Su's special praise because of not only its exquisiteness but also the pervasive explanations as follows.

As we know, lyrics, emerging in the period from the late Tang to the Five Dynasties, are mainly composed in euphuistical and flowery language for recreation and entertainment activities. Depictions on beauties, scenery and sentimental mood were the dominant themes of the lyrics in the early Song Dynasty. It was not changed until Su Shi made a debut, broke the monopoly of the conventional style and created a new high in style reform.

*The Masterpiece of a "Veteran Fox"*
*– Appreciating Wang Anshi's Fragrance of Laurel*
*Branch: In Memory of the Ancient Capital*

For instance, in the *Charm of a Maiden Singer,* Su presented a brand new lyrical pattern which integrated landscapes, history and figures with a bold and generous mind.

Thus, Su Shi evaluated others based on his own aestheticism instead of traditional taste. So, while reading this lyric by Wang Anshi, one of the few lyrics qualifying Su's aesthetic standard at that time, Su must have the feeling "great minds think alike." Both Wang's abandonment of the outdated style of the Five Dynasties and Su's discard of the feminine themes are extraordinary revolutions in lyrical history. Thus, the anecdote that Su called Wang "a veteran fox" is also a recognition of Su himself.

Lyrics, as a musical literature, focus on tune. According to famous female lyricist Li Qingzhao, both Su Shi and Wang Anshi are unqualified lyricists in tune. However, in the aspect of theme, they both were exceptional lyricists with innovative conceptions. Their depictions, unconstrained in patterns and plain in diction, are concise, connotative and comprehensive.

The lyric, whether in expressing emotion or in praising landscapes, can grasp the essence instead of all-inclusive presentation. This is why Su praised the work by Wang.

In the lyrical history, the lyric by Wang, like those by Su, is an example to break the conventional concept "lyrics for recreation." It is also a proof that Su and Wang were "bosom friends in writing."

*Su Shi Comes Back to the Imperial Academy* by Zhang Lu of the Ming Dynasty

# A Natural Expression of Emotion
## – About Ouyang Xiu's *Song of Hawthorn*

Zhao Qiping

In the Southern Song Dynasty, Zhang Shunmei, a handsome scholar from Yuezhou, met a loving girl on the Lantern Festival. They made an appointment on the next day and intended to elope together. But, they lost touch with each other in the crowded lantern parade. Later on, Zhang learned of the girl was dead by mistake, and fell into illness. Alone in the chamber, Zhang read the lyric *Song of Hawthorn* by Qin Guan, saying:

*Last year on lunar festive night,*
*Lanterns' mid blooms shone as daylight.*
*The moon rose atop willow tree;*
*My lover had a tryst with me.*

*This year on lunar festive night,*
*Moon and lanterns still shine as bright.*
*But where's my lover of last year?*
*My sleeves are wet with tear on tear.*

But, after some hardships, Zhang finally had a reunion with the girl.

It was a popular story in ancient China and reflected the profound influence of the lyric *Song of Hawthorn*.

Lantern Festival, similar with the Spring Outing, has been a conventional dating occasion for the youth since the Tang Dynasty and often appeared in literature. The said story is a reflection of realistic life, so is the description in the *Song of Hawthorn*.

However, the lyric was not composed by Qin Guan as the story said. It was also not authored by Zhu Shuzhen or Li Qingzhao as some critics said. Actually it is a work of Ouyang Xiu. Known as a master of Confucianism and a literati leader, Ouyang Xiu, was open-minded and effusive in creating love lyrics. His lyrics were neither hypocritical in describing the love nor satirical in exposing the decadence of the aristocratic life. The *Song of Hawthorn* is such a representative work.

Portrait of Ouyang Xiu

*79*

Most lyrics on Lantern Festival in the Song Dynasty are on the festive entertainment and recreation to gild prosperity and peace and whitewash the odious situation. In the Song Dynasty, there are few works on romances on Lantern Festival, and fewer on straightforward description of the emotion. And, the lyrics comparable with Ouyang Xiu's *Song of Hawthorn* can be counted on fingers.

The *Song of Hawthorn* reflects a folk custom and represents in a ballad style. We can find the origin of "The moon rose atop willow tree; My lover had a tryst with me" and similar writing techniques in the ancient *Book of Songs (Classic of Poetry, Shi Jing)*. The contrast between "last year" and "this year," between "tryst" and "separation" is a frequent expression in ballads employed by scholars. In addition to guiding the showy and frivolous lyrics prevailed in the Five Dynasties to elegance and comeliness, Ouyang Xiu also strengthened the connections between lyrics, ballads and folk songs.

Because of the influence of folk works, Ouyang Xiu was good at describing the girls cherishing fond dreams of youth, love and life and presenting their innermost delight and sorrow in pursuit of love. Moreover, the trim diction and intentional repetition in the lyric show the beauty of rhythm, such as the contrast of "last year on lunar festive night" and "this year on lunar festive night" , "lanterns' mid blooms shone as daylight" and "moon and lanterns still shine as bright," at the 1st and 2nd stanzas

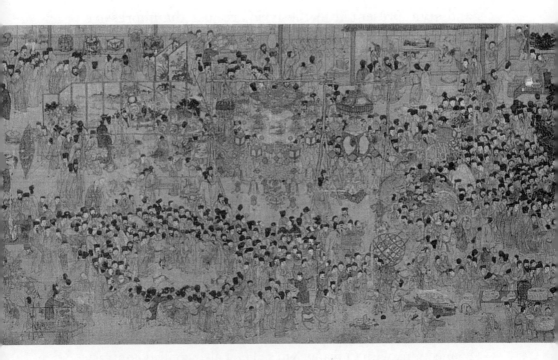

*The Lantern Festival* in the Ming Dynasty

respectively. Especially, the sharp contrast between "my lover had a tryst with me" and "but where's my lover of last year" vivifies the rise and fall of the lyricist emotion and embodies the lyricist innermost fluctuations in several lines. The natural, fresh, euphemistic and graceful diction and style presented in the lyric are just the impressive characteristics of folk songs.

Despite of the orderly diction and the complex presentation, the *Song of Hawthorn* recalls the past in the 1st stanza and depicts the present in the 2nd stanza. In addition to the sharp contrast with different images in the two stanzas, more importantly, the lyricist expressed distinct moods in the stanzas. Both Li Shi and Xin Qiji imitated this lyric of Ouyang Xiu with swallows as the image. But they two focused more on the relationship between a person and swallows, which was inferior to Ouyang Xiu's presentation of the relationship between persons, i.e, love.

However, the lyrics by Li Shi and Xin Qiji had connections with Ouyang Xiu's. They also applied contrast between the same image at different time and locations to describe the changes in life. Similarly, contrast between different images is also popular in poems and lyrics to highlight the season. While, the contrast between the same image, like in this lyric, highlights the change of people with the constancy of the scenario, and the innermost depression of the lyricist accordingly. Natural images often

*A Happy Family Reunion* by Yao Wenhan of the Qing Dynasty

83

arouse the change of people's mood. But people, instead of a passive acceptance, also associate their life experience with the changes while enjoying the nature. In lyric and poem creation, it is called "describing scenery with emotion." The author observes the object, thus the object contains the author's moods.

The protagonist in this *Song of Hawthorn* should be a young girl who had a date with her sweetheart on the Lantern Festival of the previous year when lanterns' mid blooms shone as daylight. The word "rose" in "the moon rose atop willow tree; My lover had a tryst with me" was sometimes written as "was" by mistake. "Rose" is a vivid depiction of the spatial and time change as well as the implication of the eager expectation of the couple. Through sharp contrast with the first stanza, the final lines "but where's my lover of last year? My sleeves are wet with tear on tear" shadow the blooming flowers, the dazzling lanterns, the bright moon and the swinging willows, and create a bleak and plaintive atmosphere. In face of the same scenario, the lyricist made a natural expression of joy and sadness. Therefore, the *Song of Hawthorn*, despite of blames of "stirring up the desire and passion" in some periods, has produced a comprehensive influence and even been quoted to the stories chanting free love.

*Emperor Qianlong Celebrates the Lantern Festival in the Court,*
Qing Dynasty

# Delineating Deep Love with a Blooming Brush
## — On the *Green Jade Cup* by He Zhu

Zheng Min, Ge Peiling

The *Green Jade Cup* is a masterpiece of He Zhu, a renowned lyricist in the Northern Song Dynasty. The debut of the lyric received high praise and great popularity as an "unparalleled work." Now, let's enjoy it!

**Tune: Green Jade Cup**

*Never again will she tread on the lakeside lane.*
*I follow with my eyes*

*The fragrant dusts that rise.*
*With whom is she now spending her delightful hours,*
*Playing on zither string,*
*On a crescent-shaped bridge, in a yard full of flowers,*
*Or in a vermeil bower only known to spring?*

*At dusk the floating cloud leaves the grass-fragrant*
*plain;*
*With blooming brush I write heart-broken verse again.*
*If you ask me how deep and wide I am lovesick,*
*Just see a misty plain where grass grows thick,*
*A townful of willow down wafting on the breeze,*
*Or drizzling rain yellowing all mume-trees!*

It is a love lyric. Since the work was composed in the lyricist's late years, it was often believed for expressing something else in the name of love. He Zhu, alias He Fanghui, was born in a noble family in Weizhou (Today's Jixian County, Henan). He had taken a military position in his early years, and shifted to civil service posts, including the lawsuit administrator in Sizhou, in his 40's. He retired in Suzhou in his late years. Through his life, he had been taking the low positions and feeling gloomy. Thus, he alleviated the political frustration with appreciation of scenery and beauties.

"Never again will she tread on the lakeside lane" describes the lyricist's great distraction because he didn't see the gone girl come back.

*Se* (a twenty-five-stringed plucked instrument, somewhat similar to the zither)

The lines "with whom is she now spending her delightful hours, playing on zither string" borrowed the image and connotation in the poem *Zither (Jin Se)* by Li Shangyin to intensify the sentimental atmosphere of the lyric. The lines "On a crescent-shaped bridge, in a yard full of flowers, Or in a vermeil bower only known to spring" vivify the loneliness and depression of the secluded lyricist in a devious, connotative and repeating way. These lines were the sighs of the lyricist for his experience. In another lyric composed in his late years, He Zhu wrote, "making heroic friends in my ambitious youthhood ... sighing for the landscape, playing the seven-string zither, seeing off the swans gone away." Despite of the difference in style, the two lyrics share a constant emotion.

The "blooming brush" in the line "with blooming brush I write heart-broken verse again" refers to the anecdote about Jiang Yan, a talented writer, who returned the blooming brush that helped him writing significant articles to its owner Guo Pu, and then could not write good pieces any more. This line is an exposure of the lyricist's depression on no opportunity to use his talent and confidence in his great ability.

The aforesaid lines are direct narration of the lyricist's distress and suffering, which are moving and affecting. However, the lyricist was not satisfactory with the direct narration and strove to highlight the emotion in a more powerful mode. The question and figurative reply at the lyric's end achieve this intention: "If you ask me how deep and wide I am lovesick, Just see a misty plain where grass grows thick, A townful of willow down wafting on the breeze,Or drizzling rain yellowing all mume-trees!" "Grass", "willow" and "rain" are familiar scenery in life. But the lyricist added impressive modifiers, such as "misty", "townful" and "drizzling" etc., for these images to cover all time and all space. With the modification, the lovesickness is universal, boundless, irresistible and unavoidable. These typical images are collectively employed to describe the lyricist's irresistible lovesickness. These moving descriptions by He Zhu conquered the readers who even named the lyricist after the lyric at that time.

The analysis indicates that the lyricist expressed his seclusion and depression by means of the lovesickness to a beauty. The profound and natural description, especially the extraordinarily depiction of the distraction and perplexity, has received exceptional praise of the readers.

*Mountains and Waters in Rain* by Sun
Kehong of the Ming Dynasty

The lyric is renowned for its flowery language, gorgeous style, refined and finger-popping diction and the skillful and appropriate application of literary quotations. It also applies the sharp contrast between the beautiful scenery and the depressive mood to intensify the deep lovesickness. The lyric presents vivid images and exquisite artistic conception. The famous poet Huang Tingjian, He Zhu's contemporary, praised him highly, "Across southern China, He Zhu is the only capable one that can compose heartbroken verse."

Noticeably, two rhetoric questions are applied in the first and second stanzas, respectively, to vivify the lyricist's mood fluctuating like a turbulent river. The answers follow the questions are the most brilliant parts that impress readers deeply.

The lyric is also noted for its novel, appropriate and diverse application of images. The transformation of abstract emotion to visual images is not invented by He Zhu. But He Zhu improved the skill to an unprecedentedly novel and wonderful level based on the creation of his ancestors. According to Critic Luo Dajing's opinion in *Crystal Lines in Poetry (He Lin Yu Lu)*, Du Fu and Zhao Gu applied "mountains" as image for depression; Li Qi, Li Yu and Qin Guan employed "waters" as image for gloominess. And He Zhu said, "If you ask me how deep and wide I am lovesick, Just see a misty plain where grass grows thick, A townful of willow down wafting on the breeze, Or drizzling rain yellowing all mume-trees!" Of all the creations, He Zhu's images are the greatest in novelty and connotation.

# A Masterpiece throughout the Ages
## *— Charm of a Maiden Singer: Ode of Red Cliff* by Su Shi

Yuan Xingpei

**Tune: Charm of a maiden singer**

*The endless river eastward flows;*
*With its huge waves are gone all those*
*Gallant heroes of bygone years.*
*West of the ancient fortress appears*
*Red Cliff where General Zhou won his early fame*
*When the Three Kingdoms were in flame.*
*Rocks tower in the air and waves beat on the shore,*

*Rolling up a thousand heaps of snow.*
*To match the land so fair, how many heroes of yore*
*Had made great show!*
*I fancy General Zhou at the height*
*Of his success, with a plume fan in hand,*
*In a silk hood, so brave and bright,*
*Laughing and jesting with his bride so fair,*
*While enemy ships were destroyed as planned*
*Like castles in the air.*
*Should the soul revisit this land,*
*Sentimental, it would laugh to say:*
*Younger than me, You have your hair turned grey.*
*Life is but like a dream.*
*O moon, I drink to you who have seen them on the*
*stream.*

The lyric intends to express the lyricist's emotion through historical figures and events instead of to recall the Red Cliff Battle, despite of its elaborated description on the scene of Red Cliff and the demeanor of General Zhou Yu.

The lyric starts from the Yangtze River flows by the Red Cliff: "The endless river eastward flows/With its huge waves are gone all those/Gallant heroes of bygone years." The eastward river and its huge waves are both a view description and a metaphor for the elapsed time. Standing by the river, Confucius once made a sigh, "It passes on just

93

like this, not ceasing day or night!" In front of the Yangtze River on the Red Cliff, Su Shi had a natural association between the flowing water, the passed eras and the brilliant figures and celebrities in history. But, how many people can experience the test of history and establish their fame over the time? General

Portrait of Su Shi

Zhou Yu of the Three Kingdom Period is one of them. Distinct with conventional verse on landscape, the lyric starts with a majestic view on the grand river, the historic events and the infinite sighs. It gives us a feeling that the lyricist stands on a historical high to compose the piece.

From the river, the lines "West of the ancient fortress appears/Red Cliff where General Zhou won his early fame/When the Three Kingdoms were in flame" come to the Red Cliff and the renowned General Zhou. Actually, when composing the lyric, Su Shi was in Huangzhou and under demotion. The Red Cliff he visited was not the one where General Zhou defeated his enemy. Su Shi regarded it

*Red Cliff* (Part)

where General Zhou defeated his enemy. Su Shi regarded it as the battlefield just for expressing his meditation over the past. General Zhou refers to Zhou Yu who established his name in the Red Cliff Battle which set a rudimentary base for the later three kingdoms.

Then comes the lines on the scenery: "Rocks tower in the air and waves beat on the shore, Rolling up a thousand heaps of snow." From the air to the shore, the verse delineates a panoramic picture and naturally ushers the historical figures of the Red Cliff into the lines "to match the land so fair, how many heroes of yore/Had made great show!" In the Red Cliff, Zhou Yu was a hero among a galaxy of stars who jointly created the magnificent history.

The second stanza concentrates on the description on General Zhou Yu, the commander of the Red Cliff Battle.

> "I fancy General Zhou at the height
> Of his success, with a plume fan in hand,
> In a silk hood, so brave and bright,
> Laughing and jesting with his bride so fair,
> While enemy ships were destroyed as planned
> Like castles in the air."

The lines depict Zhou Yu was a high-spirited youth and just married when commanding the Red Cliff Battle. According to historical records, when the Red Cliff Battle took place, Zhou had married for ten years. But, artistic truth doesn't equal to the reality. As a romantic lyric, it shouldn't be testified with realistic facts. The lyric was Su Shi's improvisational creation with no need to consult Zhou Yu's marriage time, the least important issue in the work. But, the bride in the line "laughing and jesting with his bride so fair" is an intentional diction of the lyricist to enrich the general's image with the beautiful bride as a foil.

Plume fans and silk hoods were popular adornments of scholars in the end of the Eastern Han Dynasty. "With a plume fan in hand, In a silk hood" presents us an elegant and calm General Zhou Yu. The verse from "I fancy...While enemy ships were destroyed as planned/Like castles in the air" is a vivid description on Zhou Yu's safe and confident victory over the enemy.

"Should the soul revisit this land, /Sentimental, it would laugh to say:/Younger than me, You have your hair turned gray." Many notes say "the soul" refers to Su Shi since he is the author for the meditative lyric. But I believe that "the soul" signifies Zhou Yu. Thus, the lines are the imagination of Su Shi. Ambitious and talented Zhou Yu reached his career culmination in his youth. So the lyricist sighed at his own destiny: despite of his ambition and talents, he had no opportunity to display, and was demoted to this historic land where he only could recall the bygones. Here, Su regarded Zhou Yu as a bosom friend who cared about him and understood his situation.

From "gallant heroes of bygone years" to "many heroes

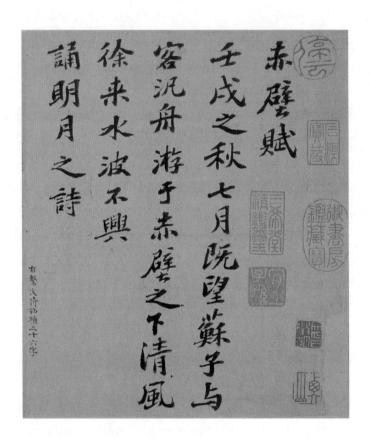

*The First Ode for the Red Cliff*

of yore" and then to the specific "General Zhou Yu", the lyric shows a clear clue on the meditation. Unexpectedly, the lyricist turned to himself, the one whose hair turned gray, from the description on Zhou Yu. So, the historical heroes including Zhou Yu served as a foil to highlight the gray-haired lyricist. The magnificent change of scenes and characters in the lyric indicates Su Shi's majestic spirit and vision.

The lyric ends with "Life is but like a dream/O moon, I drink to you who have seen them on the stream" to sigh for the transient and visional life. Comparing life with the river, the moon and the permanent nature, people will have similar sighs. In *The First Ode for the Red Cliff,* Su Shi also said "I regret the brevity of our life and envy immensity of the Yangtze River." Su Shi intended to grasp the time and establish monumental feats, but he couldn't realize his dream in the reality. Thus, the talented genius gave the sigh. "O moon, I drink to you who have seen them on the stream" is both the condolence to the bygone heroes and the pursuance for comfort from the moon. In the *Prelude to Water Melody,* Su Shi intended to fly to the moon. In *The First Ode for the Red Cliff,* Su Shi said, "Only the bracing breeze on the river and the bright moon in the mountains, which make in our ears a pleasant sound and in our eyes dreamy color, will be never spent, and may be freely used. They - the immeasurable treasure, given to us by our Creator, which you can enjoy with me." With reference to these quotations,

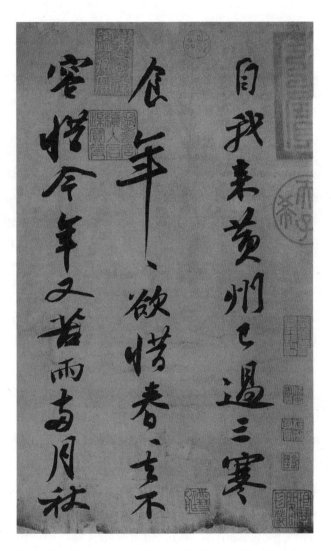

Su Shi's calligraphy of *Ode to Cold Food Festival in Huangzhou*

we may understand Su's implications better.

Tours to scenic spots or historical sites often arouse poets or lyricists' emotion on the bygones and inspire them to compose more connotative works. In these works, the combination of scenery and emotion, and the mingling of history and the reality, offer a better presentation of the authors' artistic talents. In the late Tang Dynasty and the Five Dynasties, lyric, a new literary style, started to prosper. Lyricists sought for inspirations from banquets, chambers and gardens. Till the late Northern Song, Su Shi broke through the convention and ushered in majestic themes to lyrics and composed this monumental *Charm of a maiden singer: Ode of Red Cliff*. A renowned anecdote collected in *Chui Jian Xu Lu* by Yu Wenbao of the Song Dynasty says, "Su Shi once asked a good singer: 'How do you evaluate my lyrics and Liu Yong's?' 'Liu's lyrics are composed for young girls to sing 'Moored by a riverbank planted with willow trees/Beneath the waning moon and in the morning breeze' with exquisite ivory clappers while yours are for strong men to roar out 'the endless river eastward flows' with iron clappers.' The singer replied. Su Shi doubled up with laughter at the fantastic answer." The story was often quoted to differentiate the styles of Su Shi from Liu Yong. But, besides that, doesn't it also show the public's unfamiliarity and astonishment to Su Shi's lyrics on historical meditation?

# A Talented and Ambitious Lyricist
## — On *Prelude to Six-state Melody* by Zhang Xiaoxiang

Li Yuanluo

In the Song Dynasty, Su Shi and Xin Qiji were representatives of the Boldness School and like two outstanding peaks for a century. Between the two peaks is a vast land with a galaxy of talents, such as Zhao Ding, Hu Quan, Yue Fei, Zhang Yuangan and Zhang Xiaoxiang etc., who inherited Su Shi's unconstrained style in lyrics and presented brilliant works in the eras after the southward migration of the court. Zhang Xiaoxiang was one of the most prominent lyricists in the period.

In the history of lyrics, Zhang Xiaoxiang was like an important bridge between Su Shi and Xin Qiji. As an adorer of Su Shi, Zhang once asked Xie Yaoren, "How do you evaluate me and Su Shi?" "Other people can never be comparable with Su Shi even keeping on learning for a century. But, you, full of talents, can replace Su's position after another ten-year efforts." Xie answered. Unfortunately, due to the sufferings of domestic troubles and foreign invasion, Zhang passed away at the age of 39 and had no time to make greater achievements. We don't know whether he can compete with Su Shi. But he deserved the evaluation "full of talents." Now, let's enjoy the talent's Prelude *to Six-state Melody*, the masterpiece of his 200 extant lyrics.

**Tune: Prelude to Six-state Melody**

*Looking at the boundary Huaihe River flows,*
*Exuberant grasses are as high as the fort walls*
*At the small dusts, cold gale, silent forts;*
*I felt absent-minded and depressed.*
*The incident occurred years ago,*
*Seems to be predestined,*
*And beyond our control.*
*Even the land by the Shu and Si rivers,*
*The land known for culture and peace,*
*Were captured by the Jin's troops.*
*In the land beyond the rivers,*

At the sunset there were flocks and herds,
As well as camps after camps.
At the night, the Jin's chief goes hunting
Accompanied by brisk cavalrymen holding bright
torches.
War drums they are beating;
Awakening me from sighing.

My arrows in bag,
My sword in sheath
Already covered with dusts,
Without any feats!
How time flies!
How courage fades!
As time elapses,
The land recapture seems hopeless.
With flattering dance, the court sues for peace,
Ends the frontier disputes and conflicts.
Across the border, the envoy in rich attire shuttles.
How could a power be like this?!
The civilians in the lost central plains,
Often look southward with sighs
For the brilliantly-decorated imperial honor guards.
If arriving here those civilians
They will be full of indignation and loyalties.
They will shed their tears as the rain pours.

The lyric was composed in the 2$^{nd}$ year of the Longxing

Period under the reign of Emperor Xiaozong of the Song Dynasty (1164). In the winter of 1161, Yu Yunwen defeated the troops led by Wanyan Liang, the monarch of the Jin Kingdom, for southward attack in Caishiji. Later on, Wanyan Liang himself was killed by his subordinate. At the rarely-seen good news since the Song court's southward migration, Zhang Xiaoxiang, who was guarding Fuzhou in Jiangxi then, was very excited and filled with delight: "So glad to know the enemy was defeated at the surfy place." However, at the same time, he worried about the treacherous court. His worry became true. In 1163, Zhang Jun, after recapturing Suzhou from Jin, was defeated at Fuli for various reasons. In the next year, Song and Jin reached a peace agreement with the Huaihe River as the boundary. According to *Records of Courts (Chao Ye Yi Ji)*, Zhang Jun was the commander for the region's troops and Zhang Xiaoxiang was his chief of staff. Zhang Jun convened warriors to submit a written statement for opposing the Song-Jin peace agreement. Zhang Xiaoxiang improvised the *Prelude to Six-state Melody*, showcasing his heroic

Photocopy of *Recension of Zhang Xiaoxiang's Lyrics*

105

demeanor and extraordinary talent to the warriors.

The initial lines "Looking at the boundary Huaihe River flows, Exuberant grasses are as high as the fort walls" are magnificent and cover the whole stanza. The lines indicate the lyricist was looking into the distance from a high place. At the vast scene, the lyricist had a deep sigh. The action "looking" is critical and pervasive in the first stanza. "Exuberant grasses are as high as the fort walls" suggests that no soldiers are guarding the fort and making preparations for the war. Then, the rhythmical short phrases "the small dusts, cold gale, silent forts" stress the bleakness and desolation of the boundary environment which was thriving years ago, and unveil the lyricist's lament over the sorrowful change. "I felt absent-minded and depressed" is both a summary to the previous lines and a shift from the scene to the memory: The Jingkang Incident and the lost of the central plains in 1127 were possibly predestined and uncontrolled. Jin's barbarism was pervasive in Northern China, a cultured and peaceful land before the Jingkang Incident. Thus, the lyricist's indignation to those suing for peace was depicted through contrast. Next, the lyricist described the camps and activities of the enemy in the lines:

> *"At the sunset there were flocks and herds,*
> *As well as stations after stations.*
> *At the night, the Jin's chief goes hunting*

*Accompanied by brisk cavalrymen holding bright*
*torches.*
*War drums they are beating;*
*Awakening me from sighing."*

The sound and defiant operation of the Jin troops was a sharp contrast with the Song's "silent forts" and slack defense. Generally, the first stanza focuses on the scenery and has three impressive features. First, the lyricist presents a bird's-eye view. Second, there is a clear time sequence from "at the sunset" to "at the night". Third, the close and distant views, the general and specific views, and the daytime and night views are completely delineated in a good sequence to present a comprehensive, profound and sentimental panoramic view.

Emotion description is dominant in the second stanza. "My arrows in bag, My sword in sheath" are plain lines describing the ordinary weapons. But, then come the lines "Already covered with dusts, Without any feats!" Thus, the description makes a turn and shows the lyricist's mingled sensations. Next, the depiction shifts from the implements to the innermost feelings:

*"How time flies!*
*How courage fades!*
*As time elapses,*
*The land recapture seems hopeless."*

The lyricist had been eager to recapture the lost land, but the time flew without any pause. What an unsolvable contradiction! How deep the sorrow is! Then what are the reasons for the tragedy? The lyricist straightforwardly satirized and criticized the court's concessions and appeasement with the lines:

Portrait of Yue Fei

*"With flattering dance, the court sues for peace,*
*Ends the frontier disputes and conflicts.*
*Across the border, the envoy in rich attire shuttles."*

If making a contrast with the previous lines, it is easy to understand the lyricist's satires to the peacemakers and pains inside. The ending lines "If arriving here those civilians/They will be full of indignation and loyalties. / They will shed their tears as the rain pours" highlight the lyric's theme "indignation and loyalties" and complete the final movement of the *Grande Sonate Pathétique* with "shed their tears as the rain pours".

The lyrics by Zhang Xiaoxiang boasts the elegance and boldness in Su Shi's works and the majesty and solemnness in Xi Jiqi's pieces. In the *Lyrics Appreciation by Baixue Study (Bai Xue Zhai Ci Hua)*, Chen Tingchao said that *Prelude to Six-state Melody* was "incisive, vivid and comprehensive, and able to make readers dance." Indeed, the majestic world in a bird's view delineated in the lyric is rarely seen in the Song Dynasty. Zhang Xiaoxiang was really a talented and ambitious lyricist. Unfortunately, he was far to give full play of his talents due to his short life.

# Aesthetic Personality and Art Sublimed by Cosmic Consciousness
## – Appreciating *Charm of a Maiden Singer: Passing Dongting* by Zhang Xiaoxiang

Yang Haiming

## Tune: Charm of a Maiden Singer

Lake Dongting, Lake Green Grass,
Near the Mid-autumn night,
Unruffled for no winds pass,
Like thirty thousand acres of jade bright
Dotted with the leaflike boat of mine.
The skies with pure moonbeams o' erflow;
The water surface paved with moonshine:

*Aesthetic Personality and Art Sublimed by Cosmic Consciousness*
*– Appreciating Charm of a Maiden Singer: Passing Dongting by*
*Zhang Xiaoxiang*

*Brightness above, brightness below.*
*My heart with the moon becomes one,*
*Felicity to share with none.*

*Thinking of the southwest, where I passed a year,*
*To lonely pure moonlight skin,*
*I feel my heart and soul snow-and-ice-clear.*
*Although my hair is short and spares, my gown too*
*thin,*
*In the immense expanse I keep floating up.*
*Drinking wine from the River West*
*And using Dipper as wine cup,*
*I invite Nature to be my guest.*
*Beating time aboard and crooning alone.*
*I sink deep into time and place unknown.*

In the autumn of 1166, Zhang Xiaoxiang returned to northern China from Guilin, Guangxi due to a "calumny-caused demotion" and passed by the Dongting Lake (the interconnected Dongting and Qingcao lakes in the lyric). At a mid-autumn night, the moonlit lake ignited the lyricist's cosmic consciousness and poetic inspiration. Thus, Zhang composed the lyric, another brilliant work on Mid-autumn Festival in addition to Su Shi's well-known *Prelude to Water Melody*.

Speaking of cosmic consciousness in poems, the Tang poems *A Moonlit Night on The Spring River* and *On a Gate*

*Tower at Youzhou* will come to our mind. However, the cosmic consciousness in Song lyrics is different from that in the Tang poems. For instance, Zhang Ruoxu expressed a dreamy, piteous and perplexed mood in A *Moonlit Night on The Spring River*:

> *"No dust has stained the water blending with the skies;*
> *A lonely wheel like moon shines brilliant far and wide.*
> *Who by the riverside first saw the moon arise?*
> *When did the moon first see a man by riverside?*
> *Ah, generations have come and pasted away;*
> *From year to year the moons look alike, old and new.*
> *We do not know tonight for whom she sheds her ray,*
> *But hear the river say to its water adieu."*

In face of the permanence of the river and the moon, the poet sighed with infinite regret as well as certain fancy. It was a pure, sincere emotion with sort of naivete. In the poem *On a Gate Tower at Youzhou*, Chen Zi'ang described a profound awareness on hardships:

> *"Where, before me, are the ages that have gone?*
> *And where, behind me, are the coming generations?*
> *I think of heaven and earth, without limit, without end,*
> *And I am all alone and my tears fall down."*

With the accumulation of the comprehensive life, historical and political experiences of the scholars since the

*Aesthetic Personality and Art Sublimed by Cosmic Consciousness*
*– Appreciating Charm of a Maiden Singer: Passing Dongting by*
*Zhang Xiaoxiang*

years of the *Book of Songs (Classic of Poetry, Shi Jing)* and the *Songs of Chu (Chu Ci)*, Chen Zi'ang had a much more mature and profound meditation in the work in comparison with Zhang Ruoxu did. Meanwhile, Chen presented an intensive loneliness in the poem: "I think of heaven and earth, without limit, without end, And I am all alone and my tears fall down." However, with the social and historical evolution and the development of humankind's thought, several centuries later, the cosmic consciousness in the Song's works featured the "harmony between the heaven and human". For instance, in *The First Ode for the Red Cliff*, "Do you know the water and the moon? ... Thus, if viewed from the side of change, apparently, between heaven and earth there is no moment which doesn't change, but on the same side of constancy, apparently, all things with their lives are infinite." In the essay, the delight in enjoying the gentle breeze and bright moon breaks the border between humankind and universe, marking that some of the Song Dynasty's scholars, with Su Shi as the representative, had shaken off their previous generations' perplexity and annoyance and reached a supreme and transcendental mind state. The progress reflects both the maturity of the feudal society and the success of social contradiction-tortured scholars in finding their self-redemption and self-transcendence arms after a twisting and arduous mind pilgrimage.

In terms of characters, mind, talents and style, Zhang Xiaoxiang had many common grounds with Su Shi. Thus,

*Red Cliff* (Part)

*Aesthetic Personality and Art Sublimed by Cosmic Consciousness*
*– Appreciating Charm of a Maiden Singer: Passing Dongting by*
*Zhang Xiaoxiang*

this lyric composed during his transit of the Dongting Lake on a moonlit night after his demotion is similar to Su Shi's works in conception and mingled with Su Shi's elements of moon and water. However, as an outstanding lyricist, in addition to learning from his forefathers, Zhang had his own literature creation, unique understanding to the universe and special artistic talents in interpreting the codes of the cosmos. Based on the inheritance of Su Shi's tradition and his own lofty sentiment and vigorous vitality, Zhang Xiaoxiang created a broad, bright and boundless spiritual world in this lyric against the backdrop of the moonlit sky and the vast lake. It is a rarely-seen masterpiece in the lyric circles of the Northern Song or even the whole ancient times.

The initial lines, "Lake Dongting, Lake Green Grass, Near the Mid-autumn night, Unruffled for no winds pass", roll out a serene and majestic picture. But, actually, the Dongting Lake is rarely tranquil in middle Autumn. So, the line "unruffled for no winds pass" is the lyricist's intentional presentation of his innermost calmness to unroll the "harmony between the heaven and human" in the below instead of the description of the realistic lake. As expected, next comes the line "Like thirty thousand acres of jade bright/Dotted with the leaflike boat of mine," suggesting the delight of harmony between the exterior and interior, and the cosmic consciousness of conversion to the nature for a human-heaven harmony. The consciousness is fully expressed in the follow-up lines: "The skies with pure moonbeams o'erflow; The water surface paved with moonshine:/Brightness above, brightness below." What a pure world! What a crystal mind! The lyricist's heart was purified by the universe and vice versa. So exciting and delighted, the lyricist was intoxicated by the personified universe. He couldn't help saying: "My heart with the moon becomes one, Felicity to share with none." In face of the vast lake and the mystic moonlight, the lyricist had a feeling of great geniality and delight instead of strangeness and terror. Isn't it the cosmic consciousness of the harmony between the heaven and human? Different from Qu Yuan's depression of "I am the only clean and sober one amid the dirty and intoxicated ones" and Li Bai's anxiety of "to grasp time for joy", the lyricist Zhang Xiaoxiang experienced an unprecedented tranquility and peace in the quiet moonlit lake. These wonderful lines unveil the profound philosophy, the everlasting secret and the permanent smile of the universe in a gorgeous mode.

However, why is the marvelous world only enjoyed by the lyricist himself? Didn't he live in the secular world? As a matter of fact, when writing the lyric, Zhang Xiaoxiang just left the officialdom, the hotbed of rumors. But, thanks to his lofty personality and broad bosom, he could jump out of the trap of selfness and experience the wonder of the universe. Of course, he was not born with the transcendental experience. Only after the hardships and

*Aesthetic Personality and Art Sublimed by Cosmic Consciousness*
*– Appreciating Charm of a Maiden Singer: Passing Dongting by*
*Zhang Xiaoxiang*

sufferings in reality, had he achieved the leisure harmonious status. This is not inherent indifference nor autonarcosis. It is a refinement of sameness and communication between the subject and the object. Thus the internal contradiction was temporarily solved. Likewise, in the poem *Drunk at Lake Watch Tower on the 27th Day of the 6th* Lunar Month by Su Shi, he wrote:

> "Black clouds—spilled ink half blotting out the hills;
> Pale rain—bouncing beads that splatter in the boat.
> Land-rolling wind comes, blasts and scatters them:
> Below Lake Watch Tower, water like sky."

It is a description on both the real scene and the poet's mind experience: all storms will end if keeping being honest and optimistic. Here, Su and Zhang shared a similar spiritual journey despite of the differences in the description sequence.

The second stanza started with "Thinking of the southwest, where I passed a year,/To lonely pure moonlight skin,/I feel my heart and soul snow-and-ice-clear." The lines are about the lyricist's situation. At that time, Zhang just broke away from the one-year-long officialdom in the southwestern region. He had lived a clean and faultless life during the period. But, he was not understood and suffered unfair treatment. Here, the lyricist was a realistic people with resentfulness. However, he immediately reached a new

*After Planting Trees at a Moonlit Night* by
Tang Luming of the Qing Dynasty

Aesthetic Personality and Art Sublimed by Cosmic Consciousness
– Appreciating Charm of a Maiden Singer: Passing Dongting by
Zhang Xiaoxiang

emotional state "Although my hair is short and spares, my gown too thin, /In the immense expanse I keep floating up" due to his great optimism and inclusiveness. In an aspiring mood, he had more romantic imagination and wrote down the magnificent lines: "Drinking wine from the River West/And using Dipper as wine cup, /I invite Nature to be my guest." What a majestic manner! What a broad bosom! It is the "expansion" of the lyricist's self-awareness, the "overflow" of the lyricist's personal charm and the new cosmic consciousness with himself as the subject. Thus, the lyric reaches its culmination: "Beating time aboard and crooning alone. /I sink deep into time and place unknown." Here, the lyricist seems to forget everything completely, the honor, the wealth, the gains, the losses and even the time. At that moment, the time seemed still, the space seemed shrunk, only a lyricist "beating time aboard and crooning alone" had been in the center of the universe throughout the eras. The tranquil Dongting Lake seemed to become a banquet with Nature as the guest, and the host with a heart and soul snow-and-ice-clear to become an ambitious and generous hero...

According to historical literature, Zhang Xiaoxiang was an ambitious, talented and farsighted patriot. Once at a gathering in Nanjing, Zhang Xiaoxiang improvised the *Prelude to Six-state Melody* to sigh for the lost land, which made General Zhang Jun, a war party leader, suspend the banquet. When touring the Huangling Temple , he composed the lines "The God of Waves at sunset retains me to see/The scale-like ripples he sets free" in *The Moon over the West River*. The two anecdotes show his lofty integrity and extraordinary literary talents. In this lyric, both aspects are presented. His lofty integrity becomes crystal and clear against the backdrop of a moonlit lake, and are more solemn and profound after being sublimed by the cosmic consciousness. His novel imagination and exceptional literary talents are more vague, mysterious and beautiful after being sublimed by the cosmic consciousness. "My heart with the moon becomes one, Felicity to share with none" are the most significant and sophisticated lines. The lyricist reached the wonderful state to express his felicity of "selflessness" and "self-denial" with the free communication between himself and the world. The lyric is a masterpiece that explores the "harmony between the heaven and human" and construes it into literary images for appreciation. This lyric, an ode to lofty integrity, is another brilliant work on Mid-autumn Festival comparable to Su Shi's well-known *Prelude to Water Melody* which is an ode to the love of humankind. It is an outstanding lyric among not only mid-autumn works but also all ancient literature creations. Its significance lies in the aesthetic personality and art sublimed by the cosmic consciousness. It will have the permanent charm thanks to its contribution in spirit purification and atheism improvement.

# Expressing Tenderness with Subtle Skills
## — Analysis on Li Qingzhao's *A Twig of Mume Blossoms*

Zheng Mengtong

### Tune: A Twig of Mume Blossoms

*Fragrant lotus blooms fade, autumn chills mat of jade.*
*My silk robe doffed, I float*
*Alone in orchid boat.*
*Who in the cloud would bring me letters in brocade?*
*When swans come back in flight,*
*My bower is steeped in moonlight.*
*As fallen flowers drift and water runs its way,*

*One longing leaves no traces*
*But overflows two places.*
*O how can such lovesickness be driven away?*
*From eyebrows kept apart,*
*Again it gnaws my heart.*

The lyric is titled *Grief of Parting* in the *Hua'an Collection of Lyrics (Hua An Ci Xuan)* by Huang Sheng. It is a description of Li Qingzhao's missing of her husband Zhao Mingcheng who left hometown for study. According to *A Travel to Langhuan* by Yi Shizhen, "Zhao Mingcheng left for study after he just married Li Qingzhao. Li couldn't stand the departure and composed A *Twig of Mume Blossoms* to her husband. " The movie *Li Qingzhao* also regarded the lyric a work for seeing off, which complied with neither the context, nor the rhyme, the logic or the reality. So, the title *Grief of Parting* in the *Hua'an Collection of Lyrics (Hua An Ci Xuan)* is appropriate.

After the marriage, Li and Zhao were a happy couple with a domestic life full of academic and artistic atmosphere. Their lovesickness was understandable once they were apart from each other. Especially, Li's deep adoration to Zhao was unveiled in many of her works. The lyric is her skillful description of her deep attachment to Zhao and reflection of the young married woman's pure and enthusiastic love to her husband.

The lyric starts with "fragrant lotus blooms fade,

*Portrait of Li Qingzhao* by Jiang Geng of the Qing Dynasty

autumn chills mat of jade" to indicate that it was in a fall when lotus blooms withered and mat turned cold. In addition to time, the initial line also uses the desolate autumn to arouse the lyricist's grief, intensify the environment and serve as a foil to the lyricist's loneliness. It also signifies the quick elapse of youth, and the desolation and depression due to the departure of the beloved couple.

In terms of expression skill and connotation, the line is similar to "lotus loses its fragrance, leaves wither," the start lines of *Silk-washing Stream* by Li Jing of the Southern Tang Dynasty. But Li Qingzhao's description is more colorful and more profound. Li Qingzhao also depicted the "chill of jade mat" to combine the object, the environment with the subject and the emotion. Thus, the diction in the lines "fragrant lotus blooms fade, autumn chills mat of jade" was highly praised by Chen Tingcao of the Qing Dynasty for the exquisiteness, gracefulness, specificity and uniqueness in *Lyrics Appreciation by Baixue Study (Bai Xue Zhai Ci Hua)*.

In face of the withered lotus and the pervasive desolation, Li Qingzhao felt greater sadness for her husband's absence. How could she release herself from the depression? Neither drinking nor singing, she made a trip for the alleviation: "My silk robe doffed, I float/Alone in orchid boat." The lines vivify Li Qingzhao's lovesickness. "Floating alone" indicates that she just floats for sorrow

The West Chamber in Moonlight
from the *Pictures of Beauties* by
Fei Danyu of the Qing Dynasty

*Beauties in Dressing Chambers* by Su Hanchen of the Northern Song Dynasty

alleviation instead of for leisure or fun. But, similar with "to quench sorrow with wine ends with greater sorrow," her "floating alone in orchid boat" was not an effective way for alleviation. On the contrary, this might awaken Li's memory of rowing together with her husband. However, Li was not an ordinary woman. She didn't attribute the loneliness to her husband's departure. She believed that her husband would miss her too, and wrote:

*"Who in the cloud would bring me letters in brocade?*
*When swans come back in flight,*
*My bower is steeped in moonlight."*

Here, "who" refers to her husband Zhao Mingcheng, and "swans come back" signifies the arrival of love letters. The lines embody the deep love between the couple and Li's trust to her husband. The image of swan is clear and impressive. It is a visible expression of the arrival of love letters by means of the legend that swans can convey letters. "My bower is steeped in moonlight" describes the time, the space and the innermost delight when receiving the love letter. The letter can release her lovesickness. Behind the delight for receiving the letter are tears shed for missing her husband and her long-time expectation. Thus, Li's lovesickness was further intensified.

Li missed her husband, and believed her husband would miss her. So, the second stanza naturally rolled out:

"as fallen flowers drift and water runs its way." Here, "fallen flowers drift" symbolizes that her youth was withering like flowers, and "water runs its way" that her husband left away like the flowing water. In the line, Li sighed for the elapse of youthhood, and especially, the isolation from her beloved husband. The subtle and sincere emotion was the source for her sighs at the fallen flowers and flowing water. So comes the next lines:

> *"One longing leaves no traces*
> *But overflows two places."*

The lines clearly say that the couple are missing each other and being tortured by the lovesickness, and indicate Li's adoration and trust on Zhao. Different from narrow-minded women, Li was open-minded and considerate. Another noted lyric by Wen Tingyun on a wife's missing of her husband reads:

> *"See, in the River*
> *Pass thousands of boats*
> *Sets a splendid Sun*
> *Flows the shinning water*
> *But your coming is not in my vision*
> *My heart cries in agony again."*

Or the lines by Niu Xiji say: "I can't see the love beans, As my eyes are filled with lovesick tears."

These lines are depictions only from the angle of the wife. But, Li Qingzhao depicted the lovesickness from two angles, which was rarely seen in ancient poems and lyrics.

Then, what is Li's lovesickness look like? Here comes the answer:

*"O how can such lovesickness be driven away?*
*From eyebrows kept apart,*
*Again it gnaws my heart."*

The lovesickness could not be released. It moved from eyebrows to heart, from the external changes to internal sufferings. The lines vividly describe the emotional surges and have comparable conception with the following verse by Li Yu:

*"Cut it, yet unsevered,*
*Order it, the more tangled—*
*Such is parting sorrow,*
*Which dwells in my heart,too subtle a feeling to tell."*

According to Wang Shizhen, the line "From eyebrows kept apart, Again it gnaws my heart" comes from Fan Zhongyan's "I have no place to avoid it, neither eyebrows nor my heart." But Li Qingzhao's lines are more ordered and more vivid than Fan's.

To sum up, the lyric is a depiction of Li Qingzhao's missing of her husband. It is a rare theme in the Song lyrics and difficult to handle. However, the lyric, boasting characteristic conception and expression skills, is an artistic classic. It boasts three features: first, the love, different from one-sided emotion or complaint, is gentle, pure and bidirectional; second, the praise to love is bold and straightforward, different from the mincing expression; third, the diction is fresh and clear with perfect rhyme and antitheses, such as the typical lines "My silk robe doffed, I float/Alone in orchid boat", "One longing leaves no traces/But overflows two places" and "From eyebrows kept apart,/Again it gnaws my heart" which only can be composed by a proficient lyricist.

# On Yue Fei's *Manifold Little Hills*

Wu Xiaoru

## I. Extant lyrics by Yue Fei

In the *Complete Collection of Song Ci Poetry (Quan Song Ci)* compiled by Tang Guizhang, three lyrics by Yue Fei are included: one is under the tune Manifold Little Hills and the other two under the tune *The River All Red*. There are disputes on authorship of the most popular one *The River All Red (Wrath sets on end my hair)*. I also have doubts especially on the lines "I'll send war-chariots rough-shod/

Through the gorges of Mt. Helan" because the lines doesn't match with the historical record. As we know Mt. Helan is in Ningxia in the western region while Yue Fei actually resisted the Jin State in the northern region, so I would rather believe the lyric was composed by others in the name of Yue Fei. However the great political influence and artistic significance of the lyric is indisputable and should not be neglected. Here comes the lyric.

**Tune: The River All Red**

*Wrath sets on end my hair,*
*I lean on railings where*
*I see the drizzling rain has ceased.*
*Raising my eyes*
*Towards the skies,*
*I heave long sighs,*
*My wrath not yet appeased.*
*To dust is gone the fame achieved at thirty years;*
*Like cloud-veiled moon the thousand-mile land*
*disappears.*
*Should youthful heads in vain turn grey,*
*We would regret for aye.*

*Lost our capitals,*
*What a burning shame!*
*How can we generals*
*Quench our vengeful flame!*

*Driving our chariots of war, we'd go*
*To break through our relentless foe.*
*Valiantly we'd cut off each head;*
*Laughing, we'd drink the blood they shed.*
*When we've reconquered our lost land,*
*In triumph would return our army grand.*

It is said that another *The River All Red (Meditations On The Yellow Crane)* collected in the *Complete Collection of Song Ci Poetry* was based on the copy of Yue Fei's original writing. It is a less popular work and copied below for reference.

The Tomb of Yue Fei inside the Temple of Yue in Hangzhou

## Tune: The River All Red

*(Meditations On The Yellow Crane)*
*To spy a vista of the Central Plain,*
*From far away my eyes I strain.*
*Beyond the hazy wilderness*
*Are many wall-enclosed cities.*
*In years that had away declined,*
*There, flower-sheltered, willow-shaded,*
*Were gabled towers decorated*
*With phoenix-and-dragon designs.*
*Before the Imperial Hill were whirls*
*Of maids wearing emeralds and pearls;*
*And in the Royal Theatre, oft*
*Music and singing rose aloft.*
*But now, what can be there descried?*
*Rampant in the suburbs ride*
*Mail-clad invaders, kicking up dust*
*Like windstorms in awesome gusts.*

*What has become of our warriors?*
*They're turned to grease for blades of swords!*
*What has become of the people?*
*They're filling up gullies and fords!*
*The self-same landscape; I sign*
*That thousands of hamlets ruined lie!*
*O when, for sanction can I plead,*
*An army of crack troops to lead,*
*So as in one straight dash to cross*

*The River and the Lo, to clear*
*Up the alien, barbarous dross!*
*And then returning to, to resume*
*My Hanyang tour, then disappear*
*Astride the Yellow Crane, like fume!*

The authorship of this lyric is also difficult to identify. But the public criticism to the corrupted court life in the first stanza doesn't seem to be from a Southern Song lyricist. The exposure to the cruelty of the war and the suffering of the people is close to the thought in the Old Democratic Revolution period. Its origin is still open for verification. But it is indeed a fairly good lyric in both thematic and artistic aspects.

Then, let's come to the third one as follows.

### Tune: Manifold Little Hills

*The autumn crickets chirped incessantly last night,*
*Breaking my dream homebound;*
*'T was already midnight.*
*I got up and alone in the yard walked around;*
*On window screen the moon shone bright;*
*There was no human sound.*
*My hair turns gray*
*For the glorious day.*
*In native hills bamboos and pines grow old.*
*O when can I be back as my homebound way blocked?*

*I would confide to my lute what I have in view,*
*But connoisseurs are few.*
*Who would be listening,*
*Though I break my lute string?*

The lyric was collected in the 19th Volume of *Collections of Jintuo (Jin Tuo Cui Bian)* and generally believed a work by Yue Fei. However the lyric, distinct from the two lyrics under the The River All Red which are incisive and vivid, is short, connotative and meaningful. This is not a rare phenomenon. Renowned writers including Fan Zhongyan, Ouyang Xiu, Liu Yong and Zhou Bangyan could write both majestic poems and graceful lyrics. So, it is natural that Yue Fei expressed his depression in an euphemistic mode.

## II. Composition background of *Manifold Little Hills*

The *Manifold Little Hills* by Yue Fei was collected in the *300 Lyrics of Song Dynasty* compiled by Tang Guizhang and the *Selected Works by Famous Lyricists of Tang and Song Dynasties* composed by Long Yusheng. According to the quotations in the two books, the lines "I would confide to my lute what I have in view, /But connoisseurs are few. / Who would be listening, /Though I break my lute string?" refer to Yue Fei's disagreements with the court's suing for peace. Yue Fei's worry was clarified in the lines in the *River*

The River All Red from the *Picture of Historic and Scenic Spots in Jianghan* by An Zhengwen of the Ming Dynasty

*All Red (Hair on End)*: "What I do mind, is not to let/My young head turn white in vain,/And be gnawed by empty sorrow then."

In the *Lyrics of Dynasties (Li Dai Shi Yu)*, the introduction to the *Manifold Little Hills* is more reasonable: The Southern Song and Jin courts drafted a peace agreement to hand over Henan and Shaanxi to the Southern Song. In the third month of 1139, Yue Fei applied to visit these places with an underlying aim to spy on the enemy situation. Having learned of Yue's real intention, the Emperor Zhao Gou and the archdove Qin Hui refused Yue's application. So, Yue Fei sighed at his lack of connoisseurs at the end of the lyric. Thus, it is well-founded to conclude the lyric was created in 1139 by Yue Fei.

### III. Analysis on *Manifold Little Hills*

In the lyric, the first stanza focuses on the lyricist's physical action and the external environment, while the second stanza on the author's mental action. The lyricist combined straightforward and connotative narration to both observe the lyric's rules and forms and express his deep sorrow in an artistic mode. For instance, "In native hills bamboos and pines grow old. /O when can I see my household?" are very connotative. "Native hills" refer to Yue Fei's hometown (Tangyin, Henan) and the lost land, including Bianjing, Luoyang and other capitals and major cities, in the central plains. "Bamboos and pines grow old" signifies the lyricist's long time stay away from hometown and his missing of hometown. The bamboos and pines also symbolize those staunch patriots who had been eager to recapture the lost land. The line "my homebound way blocked" doesn't point out the subject. Actually the "homebound way" was blocked by those capitulationists in particular, including the Emperor Zhao Gou and the powerful minister Qin Hui, and the enemy as well. As this could not be directly exposed at that time, the lyricist left it to the imagination of the readers.

The starting lines "The autumn crickets chirped incessantly last night, /Breaking my dream homebound; /'T was already midnight" are actually the lyricist's feeling after awakening from a dream. "The homebound dream was broken" indicates the lyricist was under a complicated political environment and even couldn't have a good sleep. "It was already midnight" also suggests that the lyricist had a sleepless night. "I got up and alone in the yard walked around" vivifies the author's anxiety and sorrow. At the silent midnight, all people had fallen into deep sleep except the lonely lyricist. Here is also a hint foreshadowing the "connoisseurs are few" in the second stanza. The first stanza describes the chirping crickets, the broken dream, the lonely walk and the bright moon in an undulatory way, symbolizing the anxiety of the lyricist.

The second stanza depicts the mental action. "My hair

*Enjoying the Moon by a Wintersweet* by Yu Ji of
the Qing Dynasty

turns gray/For the glorious day" describes the lyricist's great ambition and efforts. "In native hills bamboos and pines grow old. /O when can I be back as my homebound way blocked?" is a depiction of his disappointment in career due to numerous obstructions. The lines "But connoisseurs are few./Who would be listening,/Though I break my lute string" borrow the anecdote on Zhong Ziqi, a renowned zither player who broke his zither after Yu Boya, Zhong's only connoisseur in the world, died. The lines express the lyricist's indignation on the absence of people who could enjoy his ambition and talents. And actually, it is the indignation that awoke him midnight, broke his dream and made him feel alone. In this way, the ending lines echo with the initial ones.

# The Lovers Part while Willow Twigs Caress the Stream
— On *Sovereign of Wine: Willows* by Zhou Bangyan

Yuan Xingpei

**Tune: Sovereign of Wine**

*A row of willows shades the riverside.*
*Their long, long swaying twigs have dyed*
*The mist in green.*
*How many times has the ancient Dyke seen*
*The lovers part while wafting willowdown*
*And drooping twigs caress the stream along the town!*
*I come and climb up high*

To gaze on my homeland with longing eye.
Oh, who could understand
Why should a weary traveler here stand?
Along the shady way,
From year to year, from day to day,
How many branches have been broken
To keep memories awoken?

Where are the traces of my bygone days?
Again I drink to doleful lays
In parting feast by lantern light,
When pear blossoms announce the season clear and
bright.
Oh, slow down, wind speeding my boat like arrow-
head;
Pole of bamboo half immersed in warm stream!
Oh, post on post
Is left behind when I turn my head.
My love is lost,
Still gazing as if lost in a dream.

How sad and drear!
The farther I'm away,
The heavier on my mind my grief will weigh.
Gradually winds the river clear;
Deserted is pier on pier.
The setting sun sheds here and there its parting ray.
I will remember long

*The moonlit bower visited hand in hand with you,*
*And the flute's plaintive song*
*Heard on the bridge bespangled with dew.*
*Lost in the past now like a dream,*
*My tears fall silently in stream.*

It has been generally believed that the lyric is on parting since Zhou Ji of the Qing Dynasty said "it is about the lyricist sees off his friend in a strange land" in the *Selected Works of Four Lyricists of the Song Dynasty (Sogn Si Jia Ci Xuan)*. In my opinion, it is a description of Zhou Bangyan's mood when leaving the capital. Having been tired of the capital life but still enchanted by his lovers there, he was reluctant to leave and recalled the bygone romances. It was rumored that Zhou Bangyan was expelled by Emperor Huizong of the Song Dynasty from the capital to other city because the latter envied Zhou's love with Famous Performer Li Shishi. The rumor, even not believable, at least indicates the lyric was composed when Zhou left the capital.

Despite of the title Willow, the lyric is not an ode to willows but the sorrow on parting. In ancient China, willows refer to parting and are often used as images for parting. This lyric is no difference. Zhou started the descriptions on shades and twigs to build the parting mood with willows.

The lines "A row of willows shades the riverside./

Their long, long swaying twigs have dyed/The mist in green" delineate the picturesque dyke along which are rows of willows with slender and gentle silk-like green twigs. In the spring mist, the willows in vagueness show a special beauty.

The said lines are the willows seen in the lyricist's current parting. But, the same willows had been seen by the lyricist before when bidding farewell to others: "How many times has the ancient Dyke seen/The lovers part while wafting willow down/And drooping twigs caress the stream along the town!" The exquisite words "drooping twigs caress the stream" vividly picture the sorrow of parting and the homesickness of the lyricist by means of the wafting twigs. Naturally, next come the lines "I come and climb up high/To gaze on my homeland with longing eye. /Oh, who could understand/Why should a weary traveler here stand?" The weary traveler who had to

Willows and Peach Blossoms in Spring by Wang Wu of the Qing Dynasty

stay after bidding farewell to his friends will feel a deeper homesickness.

Then, the lyricist comes back to willows: "Along the shady way, /From year to year, from day to day,/How many branches have been broken/To keep memories awoken?" Besides the superficial depiction to willow branches, these connotative lines are actually the sincere and significant sighs at the frequent partings in the secular world.

After building the parting atmosphere with willows in the first stanza, the lyricist expresses his own parting mood in the second stanza. The line "Where are the traces of my bygone days?" refers to the lyricist's recollection of the memories in the capital. Next comes the recollection: "Again I drink to doleful lays/In parting feast by lantern light, /When pear blossoms announce the season clear and bright." Here the word "again" emphasizes the lyricist often recalled the bygone good time.

> *"Oh, slow down, wind speeding my boat like arrow-head;*
> *Pole of bamboo half immersed in warm stream!*
> *Oh, post on post*
> *Is left behind when I turn my head.*
> *My love is lost,*
> *Still gazing as if lost in a dream."*

The lines are the lyricist's feeling when watching the riverside scenery onboard. The lyricist was reluctant to leave as his sweet heart was still in the capital so he hoped the boat to "slow down". The lines "My love is lost,/ Still gazing as if lost in a dream" represent his listless depression for the parting.

Sequentially, the third stanza depicts the sentimental trip after the parting. When the boat went farther and farther, the lyricist's grief became heavier and heavier: "How sad and drear! /The farther I'm away, /The heavier on my mind my grief will weigh." Leaving at the noon, the lyricist now arrived at a deserted pier bathed in the setting sunshine at the dusk: "Gradually winds the river clear; / Deserted is pier on pier. /The setting sun sheds here and there its parting ray." The setting sun and the deserted pier against the vast backdrop highlight the lyricist's loneliness and bleakness. He couldn't help recalling the past: "The moonlit bower visited hand in hand with you, / And the flute's plaintive song/Heard on the bridge bespangled with dew. /Lost in the past now like a dream, /My tears fall silently in stream." Those beautiful nights spent with his sweetheart in the moonlit bower or on the dew-decorated bridge are still vivid, impressive, and seem to come back like a dream and move the lyricist into tears.

To sum up, the lyric is flexuous and connotative with great underlying significance and meaningful scenic and emotional descriptions.

Zhou Bangyan, alias Meicheng, also named himself Clean and True Hermit (*Qing Zhen Ju Shi*). According to the proper comment of Liu Yongji in his *A Brief Analysis of Lyrics from Tang to Song Dynasties*, Zhou Bangyan, an adept at both music and literature, could compose lyrics with gorgeous temperament and graceful diction, thus producing considerable influence to the lyricism in the Southern Song Dynasty. This *Sovereign of Wine*, featuring "gorgeous temperament and graceful diction", has been deemed as one of the masterpieces of Zhou Bangyan. According to the comment of Shen Yifu, a lyric critic in the Song Dynasty, in *How to Appreciate Lyrics (Yue Fu Zhi Mi)*, Zhou Bangan was "exempted from any secular mercenariness." Comparing with Liu Yong's works, Zhou's lyrics are more poetic and more scholarly. This lyric, though no conversion or quotation of poetic lines, is still close to a poem in sentiment and atmosphere.

# Refine Diction, Polish Wording
## – On Zhou Bangyan's *Fragrance Filling the Hall: Summer*

Tang Guizhang

Zhou Bangyan was a master of lyrics in the late period of the Northern Song Dynasty. Being accomplished in music, Zhou created a number of lyrics under slow tunes. He was adept at delineation and elaboration of both scenery and emotion. Zhou's works were rich in styles and changes, and powerful in expression and depiction. He was deemed by Wang Guowei as a master in lyrics comparable with Du Fu in poems. His lyric *Fragrance Filling the Hall* is attached below to prove that.

149

**Tune: Fragrance Filling the Hall**

*Composed at the Wuxiang Mountain, Lishui in a summer day.*
*Wind raises the oriol's chicks, rain manures the plum sprouts, midday sun makes trees grow, clearing and rounding.*
*The ground is flat, the mountains near, wet clothes damping over the fire.*
*As man is quiet, the birds play happily. Outside the small bridge, new green in gurgling water.*
*Leaning upon a balustrade, amidst yellow gourds and withered bamboo, I ask myself if the ship will reach Jiujiang.*

*Year after year, like a migrating swallow, across the vast desert, comes under eaves.*
*But never think at outside of yourself, if long or short, reverberate the ancient.*
*Emaciated and tired are the guests from the south, let them hear music, play flutes and lutes,*
*Make a banquet on the fields; first prepare their mats and pillows, and let us only sleep when we are drunk.*

In the eighth year of the Yuanyou Period under the reign of Emperor Zhezong of the Song Dynasty (1093), Zhou Bangyan was appointed as the magistrate of Lishui County at the age of thirty-nine. Wuxiang Mountain is in

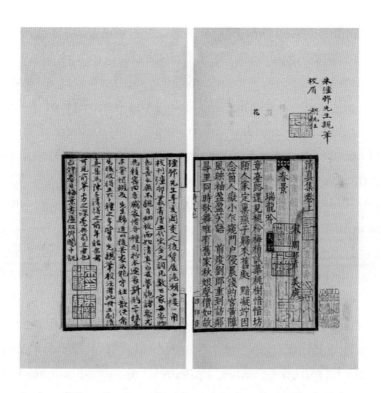

*Lyrics of Zhou Bangyan* (Produced during the period under the Reign of Emperor Guangxu of the Qing Dynasty)

the south and nine kilometers away from the Lishui county seat. There were the Wuxiang Temple and Han Xizai Reading Hall in the deep and serene mountain.

The first stanza elaborately depicts the early summer scenery in southern China. The second stanza expresses the sophisticated emotion at the scenery in a style evolved from Liu Yong's lyrics. "Wind raises the oriol's chicks, rain manures the plum sprouts, midday sun makes trees grow, clearing and rounding" describes the maturity of oriols and plums, the midday sunshine and the exuberant trees. These are the beautiful scenery of the Wuxiang Mountain in the eyes of the lyricist.

"The ground is flat, the mountains near, wet clothes damping over the fire" depict the special environment: a low-lying, humid, mountainous region with luxuriant trees. The diction is concise, vivid, impressive and refined.

The line "As man is quiet, the birds play happily" describes the admirable free life of birds to reflect the lyricist's depression. And "Outside the small bridge, new green in gurgling water" indicates the humid climate in a tranquil low-lying place.

The lines "Leaning upon a balustrade, amidst yellow gourds and withered bamboo, I ask myself if the ship will reach Jiujiang" indicate the lyricist's view angle in "leaning upon a balustrade" and his demotion status in "yellow gourds and withered bamboo" which are renowned images for relegation by Bai Juyi in *Ode to a Pipa Singer.*

Next the lyricist assimilates himself to a swallow in the lines "Year after year, like a migrating swallow, across the vast desert, comes under eaves", hinting his rough officialdom career.

"But never think at outside of your self, if long or short, reverberate the ancient" persuades the people to withdraw from the chaos and seek for a pleasant life. The lines "Emaciated and tired are the guests from the south, let them hear music, play flutes and lutes" suggest the underlying sorrow and pains in addition to the banquet in a majestic mode.

The lines "make a banquet on the fields; first prepare their mats and pillows, and let us only sleep when we are drunk" indicate the lyricist's endless sorrow and intention to evade through hangover and sleep.

In the second year of the Yuanyou Period under the reign of Emperor Zhezong of the Song Dynasty, Zhou Bangyan left Bianjing and started offices in remote regions like Luzhou, Jingnan and Lishui. He often sighed at his career, which was also revealed in the lyric in a connotative mode. The first stanza is the elaboration of the scenery and the lyricist's subtle feeling and innermost agonies through his application of the demotion images "yellow gourds and withered bamboo". In the second stanza, he assimilates himself as a migrating swallow to reflect his floating life. He also intends to drown the sorrow in cup but only ends with a sleep for a transient tranquility.

According to Chen Zhensun, Zhou Bangyan was adept in quoting and converting Tang poets' lines and presenting a gorgeous and exquisite elaboration. In this lyric, Zhou converted lines of Du Fu, Bai Juyi, Liu Yuxi and Du Mu etc. and improved their verse to perfection. The refined diction and graceful wording make the lyric an outstanding masterpiece.

# Thousands of Words Sealed at the Tongue Tip
## – On *Phoenix Hairpin* by Lu You

Zhou Xianshen

Red soft hand, yellow-cover wine, spring came amidst willows draped over walls.

Wicked east wind, short-lived joy, leaves a pining heart, and lonely years befall.

Wrong! Wrong! Wrong!

Spring comes and goes, as you waste away; your tears must have soaked many a handkerchiefs.

Peach blossoms fall, by the lonely pond and buildings, our vows intact, yet we can't connect.

Forget! Forget! Forget!

*Phoenix Hairpin* is about the tragic love and marriage of the poet. Deep sadness can be felt between the lines. That's why the poem has been greatly influential for generations. It was even adapted for operas and movies.

The young poet, Lu You, got married with a girl whose family name was Tang. They loved each other deeply. Tang showed great filial obedience to Lu You's parents. However, this did not help her win the favor of the mother-in-law, who finally managed to force the couple to divorce. Later, both Tang and Lu You remarried, even though they still loved and missed each other very much. One day, during a spring outing, Lu You met with Tang in the Shenyuan Garden located south of the Yuji Temple in Shaoxing. Tang entertained him with wine. Lu You was greatly moved. He recalled the past and felt very sad. So he wrote the poem on the wall of the Shenyuan Garden. It is said that Tang died of depression for her unfortunate love shortly after their encounter. (See Volume X, *Qi Jiu Xu Wen*, by Chen Hu (Song Dynasty); Volume I, *Qi Dong Ye Yu*, by Zhou Mi(Song Dynasty); which are largely identical in content despite minor differences.)

Lu You loved Tang very much and felt very sorrowful about their ill-fated love and the death of Tang. He could never forget Tang. He wrote a poem about their encounter at the age of 68 (1192). The preface for the poem said, "It was the Shenyuan Garden, south of the Yuji Temple. I wrote a poem (namely the *Phoenix Hairpin*) on the wall forty years ago. I visited it again later, but the owner of the garden had changed for several times. I read the poem and felt so frustrated."In 1199, the 75-year-old poet wrote another two poems under the title of "Shenyuan Garden" to mourn for Tang, which are very famous, too. Part of the poem said, "My tears drop following your traces, even though I will soon die and be buried at the foot of the Jishan Mountain." Lu You had never forgotten Tang and their tragic love and marriage due to the feudal ethical codes as well as the poem about their love through his life.

There are different opinions on when the poem was written. In accordance with the preface mentioned above, it should be written by the poet at the age of 28. However, in accordance with the Volume I of *Qi Dong Ye Yu* by Zhou Mi, it should be written in 1155, when the poet was 31 years old. Even so, it can be sure that the poet was quite young when he wrote it.

The first part of the poem is to recall the past, which was then associated with the current life, indicating the great resentment against the feudal ethical codes that forced them to part from each other. The first three sentences are about the recall of their life before separation. "Red soft hand, yellow-cover wine, spring came amidst willows draped over walls." It described the scene that they had a joyful spring outing together. "Red soft hand" refers to rosy and delicate skin of the lady. It actually refers to the beauty of Tang. It is the subjective

Portrait of Lu You

feeling of the poet, naturally showing his love for Tang. "Yellow-cover wine" refers to a kind of official wine covered by yellow paper. It is not about drinking. Instead, it aims to form up contrast of colors to indicate the joyful atmosphere. "Spring came amidst willows draped over walls."Such a short sentence informs the time (spring), location (a famous garden, but not have to be the Shenyuan Garden) and the environment (bright and beautifulspring scene with red flowers and green willows) of the outing. It draws a picture with bright and clear color and cheerful and delightful atmosphere and conveys the fervent love between the couple.

Then, the tone turns. From far to near, it describes the life from the past to present. "Wicked east wind, short-lived joy, leaves a pining heart, and lonely years befall". "East wind" implies the rude power forcing them to part from each other. It may refer to Lu You's mother. "Wicked" was used to show the emotional tendency of the poet. It shows the psychic trauma suffered by the poet due to the ruthlessness of his mother. Mao Jin (Ming Dynasty) said that the poem shows the filial piety of the poet to his parents and the love for his ex-wife at the same time (*Ci Lin Ji Shi*). It should not be correct. This sentence just refutes it. Lu You had several poems written after hearing the sound of Gu'e (which is a kind of waterfowl, which, as legend said, was changed from a woman who died of abuse by her mother-in-law). It shows obvious hatred of abuse by mother-in-law. It is not possible that there is no relevance with the experience of the poet himself. The poem does not straightforwardly show the object against the feudal ethical codes and patriarchal system. However, it implies strong resentment from the heart of the poet. From the tone to the implications, the phrase of "wicked east wind" leads to thethree following sentences. The "wicked east wind" resulted in the "short-lived joy", "a pining heart" and "lonely years". Then, based on strong emotional expression, the poet used the "Wrong! Wrong! Wrong!", a repeated way to express complicated feelings: the resentment against the ruthless east wind, the regret for his submission and the sorry for their separation. It vividly and strongly shows the sorrow and resentment of the poet.

The second part of the poem focuses on expressing the resentment and pain for the separation. The poet further expressed his resentmentthrough the expression of his love and sympathyfor his ex-wife. "Spring comes and goes, as you waste away; your tears must have soaked many a handkerchiefs."These sentences are about the encounter. Tang was gaunt and obviously in pain. "Spring comes and goes."It corresponds to and forms up contrast with the scene that "spring came amidst willows draped over walls", meaning that the spring was as beautiful as it used to be while the appearance of the people had changed after years of suffering from sadness since their separation. The expression of "waste away"containsabundantand deep feelings of the poet. Obviously, she got much thinner due to the pain from separation and the depression from lovesickness. However, can anything change because of her self-torture?So, he said that "you waste away", showing his unlimited tender affection and comfortfor Tang and his sadness and resentmentfor that he could do nothing for the reality and even could not tell his pain to anyone. "Your tears must have soaked many a handkerchiefs."When writing this sentence, the poet tried to express the feelings through tangible things. It leads us to the picture that the innocent lady tears every day after parting from her ex-husband due to the persecution of the feudal ethical codes.

The four sentences following that further indicate the melancholy and pain for the change and separation. "Peach

Shenyuan Garden

blossoms fall, by the lonely pond and buildings, our vows intact, yet we can't connect."The fallen peach blossoms may be description of the reality and alsosymbolization, which is connected with the "wicked east wind" mentioned above, meaning that the gorgeous and lovable peach blossoms had fallen due to the destruction of the ruthless east wind and indicating the resentment against east wind and the sympathy for peach blossoms. The "lonely pond and buildings" is also an obvious contrast to the happy time in the past, meaning that the same pond and buildings now seemed lonely and sad, with implication that both the poet and his ex-wife were in no mood to enjoy the flowers. The word "lonely" completely shows the loneliness and sadness of the poet. The two sentences following that means that both of them were unswervingly loyal to their love, but, are the vows enough? They still had to part. It was even hard to meet again, let alone communication! It reflects the dilemma faced by the young couple who lacked resistance against the feudal ethical codes and patriarchal system and their helplessness and pain.

The poem is ended with "Forget! Forget! Forget!", as echoes to the "Wrong! Wrong! Wrong!".It conveys abundant, strong and profound emotions. It means "Stop! Stop! Stop!", showing the helplessness and pain in an intensified way with complicated content. Why did he want to forget it? Was the poet suggesting Tang to forget all? Obviously, they love each other so much that thorough break was impossible. Then, was the poet trying to persuade his ex-wife and also himself to forget the resentment and pain? The sentence may contain all these meanings, but not exactly. It shows the mental contradiction, which cannot be clarified even by the poet himself.

The poem, full of strong emotions, reads sentimental and sorrowful and shows the deep and lingering love of the couple. The emotions behind the words can be felt after repeated recitation. It boasts strong artistic appeal, which does not lie in free expression of emotions but in what was unspoken. That's why Wu Mei said that "thousands of words sealedat the tongue tip" when commenting the poem in his work titled *Shuang Ai San Ju.*

In accordance with the Volume X of *Qi Jiu Xu Wen* by Chen Hu of Song Dynasty, Tang also wrote a poem after reading the poem, saying that "a pitiless world, hard-hearted people". Unfortunately, the complete original work was not passed down. The *Poetry*, the Volume 118 of *The Imperial. Selection of Poems of all Generations* (Qing Dynasty), quoted the words of the Owner of Kua'e Study, which includes the complete poem by Tang. However, most people believe that it is the version supplemented by later scholars. Here below is the poem for reference:

*A pitiless world, hard-hearted people, the evening rain beats petals down.*

*Eveningwind dries, not the tears; I want to write, but can only lean on the fence.*
*Tough! Tough! Tough!*
*We parted ways, yesterday has gone, and sickness haunts like a hanging rope.*
*The horn is chilling, and the night is long; shunning questions, I dry my tears and feign joy.*
*Hide! Hide! Hide!*

# On Several Lyrics by Xin Qiji

Nie Shijiao

The lyrics by Xin Qiji boast not only unrestrained style but also rich contents concerning patriotism and rural lifestyle and customs which were seldom touched by his precursors. Xin was unique and original in observing and describing rural lifestyle and customs and often more competent than his peers in this field. Now, let's have an analysis on Xin's rural life lyrics as follows.

First, Xin's description to rural life is more vivid, more exquisite and more subtle than others' works. Xin's work is just like a rural genre painting. For instance, the well-known *Pure Serene Music: Village Life* is a representative work:

**Tune: Pure Serene Music**

*The thatched roof slants low,*
*Beside the brook green grasses grow.*
*Who talks with drunken Southern voice to please?*
*White-haired man and wife at their ease.*

*East of the brook their eldest son is hoeing weeds;*
*Their second son now makes a cage for hens he feeds.*
*How pleasant to see their spoiled youngest son who heeds*
*Nothing but lies by brookside and pods lotus seeds!*

What a vivid description! The low thatch, the clear brook, the lovable old couple and their sons are all lively depicted. Liu Houcun wrote a poem of similar theme. But Liu's work is far below Xin's in vividness and vision angle. Xin's description shows his delight on the rural life.

Second, Xin highlighted his own personality, experience and ideal in his lyrics. For example, different with other one's description on drunkenness, Xin composed the lyric below in the *Tune: The Moon over the West River*:

*Drunken last night beneath a pine tree,*
*I ask if it liked me so drunk.*
*Afraid it would bend to try to raise me,*
*"Be off!" I said and pushed its trunk.*

The Portrait of Xin Qiji collected by the Xin's Family at Xishan, Qianshan County, Jiangxi Province.

Here, Xin indicated that his personality was more lofty than the pine tree, a general image for loftiness in China. Similarly, he assimilated himself as a pine tree enwound by vines and presented a spirit to shake off the secular fetters.

Third, Xin's lyrics are rolled out from a story through high recapitulation. On the marriage theme, Bai Juyi focused on the closed, primitive life and the rural marriages in a lengthy and narrative way. But Xin summarized the marriage in a closed village just in one line "the daughters in the small village are married to either Yu or Zhou."

Last, Xin's rural lyrics are not pure description on natural scenery. He often described secular customs to present a greater reality sense. As for literature works, the depiction of secular customs is more important than that of natural environment due to the former's contribution to authenticity. Xin attached special emphasis to secular customs in his works. Let's compare Xin's work with that of Wang Jia, a poet in the Tang Dynasty. For instance, in the depiction to spring, Wang Jia wrote in the poem *After a Spring Rain*:

> "Before the rain I still see blooming flowers;
> Only green leaves are left after the showers.
> Over the wall pass butterflies and bees;
> I wonder if spring dwells in my neighbor's trees."

The poem is a pure description on spring scenery and has no elements on customs. Different from Wang Jia, in

*The Mountains and Brooks in the Rain* by Wang Meng in the Yuan Dynasty

his *Partridges in the Sky*, Xin described spring this way:

*The tender twigs begin to sprout along the lane;*
*The silkworm's eggs of my east neighbor have come out.*
*The yellow calves grazing fine grass bawl on the plain;*
*At sunset in the cold forest crows fly about.*

*The mountains extend far and near;*
*Lanes crisscross there and here.*
*Blue streamers fly where wine shops appear.*
*Peach and plum blossoms in the town fear wind and*
*showers,*
*But spring dwells by the creekside where blossom*
*wildflowers.*

In this lyric, only the lines "Peach and plum blossoms in the town fear wind and showers,But spring dwells by the creekside where blossom wildflowers" are similar to Wang's scenic description of "Over the wall pass butterflies and bees; I wonder if spring dwells in my neighbor's trees", all others are on the secular life, such as the silk raising, spring sowing and wine shops. So, Xin's lyric is more lifelike than Wang's poem.

Lenin once pointed out, "to evaluate historic feats should not be based on whether historical figures can provide things needed in modern but whether they can provide something new in comparison with their predecessors." It is the historical materialism that should be adhered to in studying ancient Chinese writers. According to this principle, Xin Qiji's rural life lyrics have new elements and impressive features, which are inheritance and development of his predecessor's achievements, in comparison with others' works on the same theme. Therefore, Xin was a progressive lyricist in the evolution history of poems and lyrics.

*A Rural Home by a Bridge* by Yuan Yao

# On Xin Qiji's *Pure Serene Music*

Wu Xiaoru

**Tune: Pure Serene Music**

*The thatched roof slants low,*
*Beside the brook green grasses grow.*
*Drunken, who talks in Southern voice to please?*
*White-haired man and wife at their ease.*

*East of the brook the eldest son is hoeing weeds;*
*The second son now makes a cage for hens he feeds.*

*How pleasant to see the spoiled youngest son who heeds*
*Nothing but lies by brookside and pods lotus seeds!*
*(Another version: Nothing but lies by brookside and*
*watches others pods lotus seeds!)*
— Quoted from *Annals and Annotations on Xin Qiji's Lyrics*

The combination of environment and figures in the lyric is extremely natural and appropriate. It is a vivid sketch of the pure and primitive rural life. The lyricist concisely delineated the lively life of a family inhabiting in a hut by a crystal-clear brook. According to the *Explanation of Selected Tang and Song's Lyrics (Tang Song Ci Xuan Shi)* by Yu Pingbo, the lyric is a description of rural scenario: the elders are drunk, their elder sons are working and the

Annals and Annotations on
Xin Qiji's Lyrics

younger son is playing. Most of the critics believe that the lyric is an objective description of rural life. But I thought that the lyric also reflected the writer's emotion in addition to the delineation. Thus, I had my own understanding to the diction and contents of the lyric. For instance, most readers and critics believe that the old couple are *"Drunken"* in the lyric. But I thought that it was the lyricist himself who heard the southern voice in a "drunken" status, similar to the diction in his line "I used to appreciate my sword when I get drunk." In my opinion, the observation of rural life with the lyricist's "drunken" eyes is much more romantic than a sober observer's witness of a drunken couple's talk in southern dialect. Critic Xia Chengtao had the same understanding with me at this point. Likewise, "How pleasant to see" in the second stanza should be the feeling of the lyricist.

In addition, different from the viewpoint that the lyric depicts the writer's own rural life, I believe that it is a rural view the lyricist saw during his travel. Moreover, there are two versions for the final line as "Nothing but lies by brookside and pods lotus seeds!" and "Nothing but lies by brookside and watches others pods lotus seeds!" In my opinion, both versions vivify the youngest son's naughty and leisure in the same way and reach equivalent effect.

The lyric is a profile of the rural life of some leisure people, and a picture of the vitality and charm of the rural area in spring. The initial lines in the first stanza,

Statue of Xin Qiji

"The thatched roof slants low, Beside the brook green grasses grow", are the views of the lyricist seen from afar, indicating that spring comes to the countryside with infinite vitality and starts the busy farming season. Then the lyricist came closer and heard the nice southern voice of an old couple from a thatched hut. He then realized the youngsters were busy in farming outside. And thus, the lines switch to the descriptions on the young people of the family.

The second stanza describes the labor scenario of the family: "East of the brook the eldest son is hoeing weeds; The second son now makes a cage for hens he feeds." Even the underage sons are engaged in the sideline work, which serves as a foil to hint the laboriousness of the grownups. The concise sketch to the rural life gives readers plentiful space to imagine. At the end of *Partridges in the Sky*, Xin

Qiji wrote: "Peach and plum blossoms in the town fear wind and showers,/But spring dwells by the creekside where blossom wildflowers." This lyric has similar artistic effect with the *Partridges in the Sky*. The two lyrics are really different tunes rendered with equal skill.

# A Novel Lyric at a Farewell Feast
## – On Xin Qiji's *The River All Red*

Huo Songlin

*Don't pluck the Tumi blossoms, please!*
*Let spring stop and the last spring flowers be prosperous.*
*Do you still remember?*
*Like the peas were the greengages;*
*We pick them together in those days.*
*The flowery bygones are like a dream,*
*The sober eyes gaze at the wind and moon.*
*The peony laughs at me in the breeze,*
*My hair turns gray.*

*With the change of seasons,*
*Gone by has the prosperity of calami and elms.*
*In the wind and storm*
*Are the water fowls' singing still the same.*
*Blossoms faded and willows withered,*
*But, butterflies and bees are still in their surround.*
*Having no worry about the elapse of spring,*
*Except the sorrow of parting.*

This is the second lyric composed by Xin Qiji at the foy for Zheng Houqing, who would go to Hengzhou to take office. The two lyrics, boasting different features, have stood the test of time and been passed on.

The first one, under the tune *Prelude to Water Melody*, depicts the scenery and history of Hengzhou. In the *Prelude to Water Melody*, the lyricist hoped Zheng to rejuvenate the local culture, develop the local farming and sericulture, benefit the local people in Hengzhou and contribute his talents to the country development. At the end, the lyricist expressed his sentimental attachment to Zheng. The lyric is majestic and unrestrained in diction, showcasing Xi Qiji's bold style. The lyric is the words given at parting and shows the deep friendship between Xin and Zheng. But one lyric is not enough to express Xin's emotion, and he composed the second one: *The River All Red*.

Different from hackneyed and stereotyped expressions on parting, *The River All Red by* Xin Qiji is novel in view angles and imaginations. The lyric, except the ending line, doesn't mention the farewell banquet or the sentimental parting. Instead, it focuses on the scenery of the late spring and makes a deep sigh on the elapse of spring time. At the end, it comes to the parting theme. But its profound significance is far beyond the scope of parting sorrow.

The surprising starting line "Don't pluck the Tumi blossoms, please!" seem to prevent someone from pluck the flower. Tumi blossoms at late spring and early summer. People who value spring often sigh: "Spring ends upon Tumi blossoms." Here, Xin persuaded people not to pick up the blossom in order to "Let spring stop and the last spring flowers be prosperous." Surely, spring will not stop even if people "don't pluck the Tumi blossoms." But the wishful thinking shows the artistic aestheticism. This is characteristics of literature distinctive from natural sciences and other social sciences.

The initial lines just indicate it was in late spring and have no descriptions on parting. Then, it comes to the bygones: "Do you still remember? /Like the peas were the greengages; /We pick them together in those days." With the elapse of spring, the prosperity of plants, such as greengages, peonies, calami and elms, has gone away. The time can never be stopped. The line "In the wind and storm/Are the water fowls' singing still the same" indicates the arrival of summer as water fowls start to sing.

"The sober eyes gaze at the wind and moon/The peony laughs at me in the breeze/My hair turns gray" in the first stanza are echoed with "Blossoms faded and willows withered" in the second stanza to stress the change of seasons and the innermost sentiment on the elapse of spring. The lines "Blossoms faded and willows withered/ But, butterflies and bees are still in their surround" actually raise a question: why are butterflies and bees still busy when plants wither? The lines also include a connotative anecdote: "In the late Spring and Autumn Period, Confucius had been busy lobbying for rejuvenating the imperial court. Wei Shengmu didn't understand his action and asked: 'why are you busy in rejuvenating the imperial court when it is collapsing?'" Xin Qiji had his underlying intention to apply the connotative anecdote.

The aforesaid lines have no direct depiction on the parting. The lines "having no worry about the elapse of spring/Except the sorrow of parting" suddenly touch the theme and end with suspense.

The lyric depicts deep sentiments over the change of seasons and the elapse of time and attributes the reason to the sorrow of parting. It is also connotative in expressing Xin's status. Xin Qiji had adhered to fight against the Jin State and proposed a set of strategic guidelines and measures. But he suffered the suppression of the capitulationists who were dominant in the court. He was deprived from his office and had stayed idle for ten years. At the farewell banquet, he first compose the *Prelude to Water Melody* to encourage Zheng Houqing to fulfill his ambition. But, he sighed at the collapsed politics and his vague wish to recapture the lost land, and composed *The River All Red* to present the status and future of the country and his own wish and disappointment through the combination of "elapse of spring" and "sorrow of parting." His popular work *Groping for Fish* also starts with "How much more can spring bear of wind and rain? /Too hastily it will leave again" and ends with "Oh, do not lean/On overhanging rails where the setting sun sees/Heartbroken willow trees," which is a perfect match of *The River All Red* and quite appropriate for reading reference.

*Willows after a Shower* by Hong Ren of the Qing
Dynasty

# Depression Hidden in Delight
## – On Xin Qiji's *Partridge in the Sky*

Yang Muzhi

**Tune: Partridge in the Sky**

*Preface: I was drunk and wrote it on the wall of a wine shop after visiting the Goose Lake.*

*Spring comes to a field dotted with shepherd's-purse blossoms,*
*In the drizzle, looking for food in the plowed field are flocks of crows.*

*Hair turns gray even in the vigorous spring,*
*Have a drink at a wine shop in the evening.*

*A leisure life, an exquisite living,*
*Mulberries grow by the west of cattle pen.*
*A young wife, in white blouse and black skirt,*
*Visits her mother in the slack season.*

It is a lyric to express emotion through scenic description. The scenic description is specific and vivid, however the emotion expressed is not as simple as the literary diction.

The starting lines "Spring comes to a field dotted with shepherd's-purse blossoms/In the drizzle, lookin g for food in the plowed field are flocks of crows" vivify the peace and vitality of the rural life. Like a sketch, the lines delineate the picturesque countryside spring for the readers. A new year starts with everything in a new appearance. Will the spring sowing start after the drizzle? But, the lyricist's mood makes a sharp turn in the lines "Hair turns gray even in the vigorous spring/Have a drink at a wine shop in the evening." Having no way to remove his sorrow, the lyricist drown the troubles in drink. Readers can also feel the lyricist's depression from the lines.

Why was the lyricist in a low mood? The preface says "I was drunk and wrote it on the wall of a wine shop after visiting the Goose Lake" and hints the situation that the

185

Picture of Shepherd's
*Purse Blossoms*

lyricist was deprived from office and had to live a retired life in his good years. In face of the vigorous spring, the lyricist sighed at the rapid elapse of time and his failure in career. The lyricist expressed his sorrow through depicting a robust spring scene to awaken the reader's sympathy to his situation.

In the second stanza, the lyricist didn't answer whether wine could extinguish his depression. He began to delineate another rural scenery: "A leisure life, an exquisite living/ Mulberries grow to the west of cattle pen/A young wife in white blouse and black skirt/Visits her mother in the slack

*Dwelling in the Mountains*
by Gong Xian of the Ming Dynasty

187

season." Different from the distant view in the first stanza, these lines look like a close shot to the leisure and primitive rural life which constitute a sharp contrast with the lyricist's anxiety and depression in the lines "Hair turns gray even in the vigorous spring/Have a drink at a wine shop in the evening." The complicated and anxious mood of the lyricist is further stressed with the leisure as a foil.

Here comes another question. Why did the lyricist drown himself in wine if he enjoyed the rural scenery? He was fed up with the urban officialdom which was full of struggles, conflicts, lies and boasts. He believed that the beautiful spring was in the field, the brooks, and the wild flowers. He was in the pure and fresh rural area, but he still had innermost depression. Also in the contemporary period with this lyric, Xin Qiji composed a lyric under Pure Serene Music including lines "I woke up in thin quilt on autumn night; The boundless land I dreamed of still remains in sight." Actually, to recapture the boundless land was the real cause in the heart of the lyricist. But he was elbowed out to the rural region for a leisure life. He loved the leisure and tranquil rural life. But the rural life was far from the war field. He loved spring. But spring couldn't bring him new opportunity and new hope.

Therefore, we can find out that the lyric described the lyricist's depression and expressed the lyricist's pursuance through the depression. That is the emotion expressed through the scenic description.

# On Jiang Kui's *A Skyful of Joy*

Zang Kejia

**Tune: A Skyful of Joy**

*Odes to Crickets*

In the Year of Bingchen, I had a drink with Zhang
Gongfu in his Dake Hall. At the singing of crickets
from the next room, Zhang and I made odes for the
singing insects. Zhang finished first and his work
which was quite good in diction. Sauntering amid

jasmines bathed in the autumn moonlight, I was inspired and soon composed the lyric. Crickets, also called Cuzhi in Zhongdu, are battlesome insects. The rich enjoying crickets bought the insects at rather high price and raised them in ivory cases for appreciation or games.

At first I chanted a wonderful poetic prose,
Like the famous poet Yu Xin used to sing his Rhapsody of Sorrows.
Then I heard crickets chirp plaintively from the hollows,
From the bronze door ring bases,
And from the stone wells covered with mosses.
Hearing this querulous sound of crickets,
The longing woman in her private room,
Unable to sleep, got up to look for the loom.
Looking at the winding mountains on the screen,
She thought of her husband travelling.
What was her emotion in such a lonely cold evening?

I seemed to hear wailing wind
And weeping rain patter on the west window.
For whom the sound of the rain and wind now stopped, now continued,
And was accompanied with the clothes-beating sound?
Travellers feeling sad in the autumn at a forlorn inn,
And concubines in a temporary palace falling into

*disfavor with the king,*
*Would be all the more heart-broken*
*When they heard the plaintive sound of crickets in a*
*cold moonlit evening.*
*In the Book of Songs a poet wrote an impromptu*
*poem on crickets with deep feeling.*
*Children knowing nothing of the sadness of the world*
*Try to catch crickets in the dark with lights along the*
*garden wall.*
*Some scholar officials have composed the chirping of*
*crickets into music,*
*Making people of the world all the more sick.*

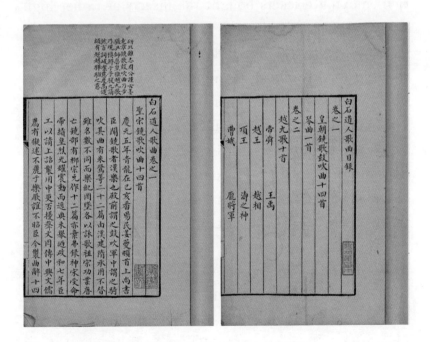

*Lyrics by Jiang Kui*

The *Ode to Crickets* by Jiang Kui has won praise of lyricists and critics over the past generations. Some people even believe this is the best work of Jiang Kui and comparable with the renowned tunes of *Hidden Fragrance, Sparse Shadows* and *Slow Song of Yangzhou.*

I enjoyed the lyric not because of its fame but because of its stir to me. People's emotion changes with the seasons. Spring makes people sentimental and autumn sorrowful. Ouyang Xiu wrote a famous *Ode to Sound of Autumn.* Sound of insects is the natural message of a bleak autumn and the inspiration for lyricists. There might be distinctive works on crickets. The preface says: "The rich enjoying crickets bought the insects at rather high price and raised them in ivory cases for appreciation." If focusing on this aspect, a lyric satirizing the rich could be composed. Also, Zhang Gongfu made an ode to crickets based on his own life experience about crickets in the same occasion with Jiang Kui. However, Jiang Kui, with few description on personal experience about crickets, put himself in the place of readers to broaden the readers' vision and communicate with the readers sincerely. This is the reason why I like the lyric.

The initial lines "At first I chanted a wonderful poetic prose/Like the famous poet Yu Xin used to sing his Rhapsody of Sorrows" set the sorrowful keynote of the lyric. The chirping of crickets are just the external factor arousing the lyricist's sorrow. Then the lyricist rolled out

蟋
蟀

*Crickets*

the description on the "querulous sound of crickets" step by step to vivify the experience. Due to the sorrowful sound, "the longing woman in her private room, /Unable to sleep, got up to look for the loom." The line "weeping rain patter on the west window" further intensifies the bleakness of the environment.

The moving lines "For whom the sound of the rain and wind now stopped, now continued, /And was accompanied with the clothes-beating sound?" naturally awaken our memories on the lines "A slip of the moon hangs over the capital; Ten thousand washing-mallets are pounding. Autumn winds keep on blowing, all things make me think of Jade Pass!" We can understand the longing woman's dilemma "If I send you winter clothes you won't be back, / If I don't, you'll suffer when cold days attack."

Then come different scenarios: Travelers feeling sad in the autumn at a forlorn inn, /And concubines in a temporary palace falling into disfavor with the king," both of which are concise, connotative, profound and moving lines make people heart-broken.

These lines make us associate the lines "He stared at the desolate moon from his temporary palace. /He heard bell-notes in the evening rain, cutting at his breast" on Emperor Xuanzong of the Tang Dynasty in the renowned *A Song of Unending Sorrow* by Bai Juyi, and "The blooming moon is rising in the evening sky. /The palaces of jade/ With marble balustrade/Are reflected in vain on the River

Qinhuai" in the *Ripples Sifting Sand* composed by Li Yu, the junior emperor of the Southern Tang, after being captured.

The lines also remind us the verse "Early to bed on journey long in rainy days /And late to rise at country inn in wind and haze" in *The Romance of the Western Bower.*

Jiang Kui often wrote short and meaningful prefaces for his lyrics. The preface introduces the occasion for the lyric and Jiang's creation process "Sauntering amid jasmines bathed in the autumn moonlight, I was inspired and composed the lyric."

Jing read Zhang Gongfu's terrific improvisation on crickets, which was based on Zhang's own life experience, and then created this novel and unique piece with the inspiration from the autumn moon and the chirps of crickets. Mingling with the "sleepless longing woman" and "the clothes-beating sound", the lyric sets up its moving and sympathetic theme.

Surely the lyricist started the work with his own experience as a lead. The lines "In *the Book of Songs* a poet wrote an impromptu poem on crickets with deep feeling./ Children knowing nothing of the sadness of the world/ Try to catch crickets in the dark with lights along the garden wall", seemingly inconsistent with the theme, are a sort of common experience and an echo with the aforesaid lines "From the bronze door ring bases,/And from the stone wells covered with mosses./Hearing this querulous sound of crickets." While the ending lines "Some scholar officials have composed the chirping of crickets into music,/Making people of the world all the more sick" echo with the bleakness in the initial lines "At first I chanted a wonderful poetic prose,/Like the famous poet Yu Xin used to sing his Rhapsody of Sorrows".

Jiang Kui and Zhang Gongfu were good friends. They drank and composed together, and won popularity with their works.

Lyric critics have distinctive opinions on Jiang Kui. On one hand, critics that emphasize on realistic significance often blamed Jiang for his excessive favor of rhyme, melody and aestheticism and lack of realistic creations composed for the society and important events. On the other hand, those in favor of aestheticism and form esteemed Jiang to the maximum. In my opinion, Jiang is different from Su Shi and Xin Qiji in style. But, his artistic accomplishments and extensive influence have been recognized. He was highly praised not only by his contemporaries including Fan Shihu, Yang Wangli and Xin Qiji but also by those in later generations.

Jiang Kui, capable for both graceful and bold pieces, boasted a unique style. No doubt, his works have enjoyed fairly high reputation and produced profound influence in the lyrical field.

# Analysis on Jiang Kui's *A Skyful of Joy*

Gu Yisheng

Jiang Kui, alias Yaozhang or Baishi, was a lyricist of the Southern Song Dynasty. *A Skyful of Joy* is one of his masterpieces and has been receiving different evaluation. According to *The Origin of Lyrics* by Zhang Yan at the end of the Song Dynasty, Jiang Kui's lyrics are the model for "elegance" and "legitimacy" and "like floating clouds without any traces." And Wang Sen, a critic in the Qing Dynasty, said that Jiang created a unique realm higher than the Gracefulness and Boldness schools. But Zhou Ji thought Jiang's works were superficially gorgeous and unworthy of reflection. Wang Guowei also sighed at Jiang's incompetency in conception. Also more blames are on Jiang's poor contents. Now, let's make an in-depth analysis on Jiang's *A Skyful of Joy*. The analysis might contribute to our understanding to Jiang's artistic achievements. The lyric says:

> *In the Year of Bingchen, I had a drink with Zhang Gongfu in his Dake Hall. At the singing of crickets from the next room, Zhang and I made odes for the singing insects. Zhang finished first and his work which was quite good in diction. Sauntering amid jasmines bathed in the autumn moonlight, I was inspired and soon composed the lyric. Crickets, also called Cuzhi in Zhongdu, are battlesome insects. The rich enjoying crickets bought the insects at rather high price and raised them in ivory cases for appreciation or games.*

> *At first I chanted a wonderful poetic prose,*
> *Like the famous poet Yu Xin used to sing his Rhapsody of Sorrows.*
> *Then I heard crickets chirp plaintively from the hollows,*
> *From the bronze door ring bases,*
> *And from the stone wells covered with mosses.*

Hearing this querulous sound of crickets,
The longing woman in her private room,
Unable to sleep, got up to look for the loom.
Looking at the winding mountains on the screen,
She thought of her husband traveling.
What was her emotion in such a lonely cold evening?

I seemed to hear wailing wind
And weeping rain patter on the west window.
For whom the sound of the rain and wind now
stopped, now continued,
And was accompanied with the clothes-beating sound?
Travellers feeling sad in the autumn at a forlorn inn,
And concubines in a temporary palace falling into
disfavor with the king,
Would be all the more heart-broken
When they heard the plaintive sound of crickets in a
cold moonlit evening.
In the Book of Songs a poet wrote an impromptu
poem on crickets with deep feeling.
Children knowing nothing of the sadness of the world
Try to catch crickets in the dark with lights along the
garden wall.
Some scholar officials have composed the chirping of
crickets into music,
Making people of the world all the more sick.
(Lyricist's Note: some scholar officials in the late
Northern Song composed Melody for Crickets.)

Lyric, an emerging poetry style at the end of Tang and early of Song, was believed a minor creation for free expression of moods. Thus, lyrics often have neither titles nor prefaces. Su Shi of the Northern Song greatly boosted the development of lyrics. Su Shi titled and prefaced his works to highlight the theme and clarify the creation background and intention. Jiang Kui prefaced his lyrics with good diction and poetic language to luster the contents. Zhou Ji criticized Jiang Kui's prefaces for the repetition of lyrical contents. The preface for the lyric proves Zhou's opinion was not correct.

Portrait of Jiang Kui

The preface introduced the creation process of the lyric. The lyric was composed in the then capital Lin'an (today's Hangzhou) in 1196. At that time, about 70 years had passed since the termination of the Northern Song. The Southern Song Court had become content to retain sovereignty over a part of the country by the beautiful Western Lake. However, patriots had been caring about the lost land, the people in the central plain and the upcoming and future challenges. At an autumn night, Jiang Kui and his good friend Zhang Gongfu (grandson of Zhang Jun, the famous general fighting against the Jin State) drank together. At the chirping of crickets, they agreed to compose under the theme. Zhang finished first and his work which was quite good in diction. Zhang vivified his childhood experience like catching crickets and cricket contests. Jiang Kui continued meditation on lines and was suddenly inspired by the autumn moon when looking into the sky. Thus, Jiang wrote the lyric. The moon, as a witness of the rise and fall of events and the vicissitudes of life, can arouse people's affluent associations. Some poems by Xie Zhuang, Li Bai, Du Fu and Lu You described the emotion when they watching the moon. It is the same with Jiang Kui who recalled the past, the travelers, the longing women and the scholars while chanting the crickets and looking up at the autumn moon. This lyric breaks the limit of ordinary odes and reflects the style and features of the times. Zheng Wenchao gave a high praise to Jiang Kui's originality while recognizing Zhang Gongfu's work in his revised *Lyrics of Baishi.* Zhang Gongfu was fairly good in diction as a competent lyricist; Jiang Kui was known for his novel style and the deep connotation in the second stanza.

At the end of the preface, it reads "Crickets, also called Cuzhi in Zhongdu (Bianjing), are battlesome insects. The rich enjoying crickets bought the insects at rather high price and raised them in ivory cases for appreciation or games." Zheng Wenchao said that it was the situation of Bianjing (Zhongdu) in the late years of the Northern Song and thus the indignation on the war-tortured society was described in the second stanza. Yu Pingbo also believed the Zhongdu referred to Bianjing. This understanding is consistent with Jiang Kui's intention. But some exegetists wrongly thought the Zhongdu referred to Hangzhou. Actually, many patriotic writers including Zhang Xiaoxiang, Lu You, Zhang Duanyi and Li Qingzhao who had been longing for recapture the central plain called the former capital Bianjing as Zhongdu in their works at that time. Then, why did Jiang Kui recall these old issues in Bianjing at the end of Northern Song? To cherish the memory? To sigh at the ups and downs? Or to reveal the reasons for the death of the Northern Song or tragedies of the times? He made no clear answer and left the questions to readers. This is consistent with his creation idea "Lines and essays have aftertaste within are the best of best" in *Baishi's Theories on Poetry*, which is different with the style of straightforward expression promoted by Bai Juyi. In this way, the preface both had internal connections and kept certain space with the lyric followed. So, the readers are eager to read the lyric after the preface and have surprising findings when reading the lyric.

The initial lines "At first I chanted a wonderful poetic prose, /Like the famous poet Yu Xin used to sing his Rhapsody of Sorrows" make a sudden start, like a peak extending to continuous mountains or a fall flowing to vast waters. Crickets chirp without emotion. But listeners feel various emotions due to their different encounters and moods. The lines indicate the lyricist, full of sorrow, sighed deeply at the chirping of crickets. It also shows that the lyric embodies the concerns on home and country and focuses on the people's responses to the chirping of crickets instead of descriptions on crickets themselves. Yu Xin was a famous poet in the late Southern and Northern Dynasties. Yu was retained in the north because his

*Along the River During the Qingming Festival* (Part) by Zhang Zeduan of the Song Dynasty

motherland Liang was terminated. He wrote numerous works including glorious pieces *Ode to Southern China* and *Ode to Withered Trees* to express his homesickness and sighs at the lost land and the miserable people. In the *Poetic Thoughts on Ancient Sites I (Yong Huai Gu Ji I)*, Du Fu wrote:

> *"The barbarian serving the ruler in the end was unreliable.*
> *The wandering poet lamenting the times had no chance to return.*
> *Yu Xin throughout his life was most miserable,*
> *In his waning years his poetry stirred the land of rivers and passes."*

Actually, these are lines to Yu Xin and to Du Fu himself. In this lyric, Jiang Kui assimilated himself with Yu Xin in a connotative way as the confrontation between Song and Jin dynasties is similar to the situation of the Soutern and Northern dynasties. The central plain was under the cruel sovereign of the Jin while the Southern Song court adhered to capitulationism. At the moonlit night, listening to the sad chirping of crickets, the lyricist made a deep sigh at the elapse of time and the hopelessness of revisiting the lost land.

"From the bronze door ring bases, /And from the stone wells covered with mosses" describes the bleakness and

*Eight Scenic Spots of Jinling* by Guo Cunren of the Ming Dynasty

205

desolation of the dismal environment. The lines "Hearing this querulous sound of crickets, /The longing woman in her private room, /Unable to sleep, got up to look for the loom" vivify the woman's actions at the sound of the insects, the messengers of winter. In ancient times, women started to make winter clothes when hearing crickets sing.

Also, Zhang Gongfu made an ode to crickets about crickets in the same occasion with Jiang Kui. However, Jiang Kui, with few description on personal experience about crickets, put himself in the place of readers to broaden the readers' vision and communicate with the readers sincerely. This is the reason why I like the lyric.

The first stanza makes a sudden end with the lines "Looking at the winding mountains on the screen, /She thought of her husband traveling. /What was her emotion in such a lonely cold evening?" At the cold autumn night, the winding mountains on the screen seem to intensify her sorrow and make her feel more depressed.

The second stanza starts with "I seemed to hear wailing wind/And weeping rain patter on the west window." The invisible and silent drizzle at the night pattered on the window, further adding the lonelines together with the clothes-beating sound from faraway amidst the insect chirping. Thus, the bleakness and loneliness were extended to the vast land, the universe and the infinity. The question "For whom the sound of the rain and wind now stopped, now continued" is also fairly meaningful. The question

*The Jianmen Pass* by Huang Xiangjian of the Qing
Dynasty

seems unreasonable, but is from the lyricist's innermost, and similar with Qu Yuan's question to the heaven, Ouyang Xiu's to the flowers and Qin Guan's to the Chenjiang River. Jiang's meditation extended with the chirping of crickets, so did the loneliness of the longing woman. However, in the war time, the situation was prevalent and the outside women by the river were also preparing winter clothes for their husbands faraway. For instance, in a *Song of an Autumn Midnight*, Li Bai wrote:

> "A slip of the moon hangs over the capital;
> Ten thousand washing-mallets are pounding.
> Autumn winds keep on blowing,
> All things make me think of Jade Pass!
> Oh, when will the Tartar troops be conquered,
> And my husband come back from the long campaign!"

In Jiang Kui's lyric, the emotion of women inside and outside the room are mingled together with the chirping of crickets and extended to travelers and soldiers in the distance.

"Travelers feeling sad in the autumn at a forlorn inn, / And concubines in a temporary palace falling into disfavor with the king" are descriptions of the sorrow, loneliness and depression of various travelers who were trapped in strange places. Readers can refer to the lines "He stared at the desolate moon from his temporary palace. /He heard bell-notes in the evening rain, cutting at his breast" on the exile of Emperor Xuanzong of the Tang Dynasty in the renowned A *Song of Unending Sorrow* by Bai Juyi. Looking at the autumn moon at the cold night, travelers fell into deep homesickness. Then comes the lines "Would be all the more heart-broken/When they heard the plaintive sound of crickets in a cold moonlit evening" which can be read with Li Bai's verse "And at last you think of returning home, /now when my heart is almost broken."

With the chirping of crickets as the clue, the lyric depicts a vast scene pervasive with hidden bitterness and homesickness. "In the Book of Songs a poet wrote an impromptu poem on crickets with deep feeling" is a powerful echo to the starting line "Like the famous poet Yu Xin used to sing his Rhapsody of Sorrows." *The Book of Songs* has lines on crickets to reflect the rural life. Here Jiang Kui also indicated the lyric was an improvisation without excessive polishing. However, the seemingly inconsistent joyful lines of "Children knowing nothing of the sadness of the world/Try to catch crickets in the dark with lights along the garden wall" suddenly rush into the sorrowful lyric. The sharp contrast highlights the bitterness of the aforesaid travelers and longing woman. It is also the connotative contrast between the capitulaitonists living a befuddled life and the patriots cherishing a hope to recapture the lost land at that time. In the Southern Song,

*Willows and Boats of the West Lake* by Xia Gui of
the Southern Song Dynasty

quite a few were content to retain sovereignty over the southern part of the country and forgot the national and household shame. Here, Jiang Kui had similar sighs with his contemporary Lin Sheng who inscribed a renowned poem on the wall of a Hangzhou hotel, saying:

*"Peaks rise beyond the peaks, while towers on towers crowd.*
*The song and dance proceed on West Lake long and loud.*
*The soft and drowsy breeze the wandering throng enchants.*
*Hangzhou, the new-found capital, their old Bianzhou supplants."*

Jiang's deep and intense pains are expressed in the ending lines "Some scholar officials have composed the chirping of crickets into music,/Making people of the world all the more sick." In the note to the lyric, Jiang pointed out that some scholar officials in the late Northern Song had composed *Melody for Crickets*. Jiang was sentimental at the social changes and made the note for analogy.

This lyric is associative, exquisite and profound, showing a colorful social reality. According to Chen Tingzchao's comment in *Lyrics Appreciation by Baixue Study (Bai Xue Zhai Ci Hua)*, Jiang's lyrics have advantages of elegance and connotation, and disadvantages of excessive application of literary quotations, and obscurity in diction. Jiang avoided the vulgarity of the early Gracefulness School but lost the school's freshness, restricted the boldness of the Boldness School and lost the school's openness. In the *Discussion on Lyrics*, Song Xiangfeng said that Jiang Kui's dicition were "full of figure of speech", for instance, "A Skyful of Joy is a lamentation for the captive emperors." In fact, when the lyric was completed, the captive emperors had been dead for decades. The paper is just an attempt to construe Jiang's lyric *A Skyful of Joy.* Opinions from all readers are highly appreciated.

# Sorrow Is a Dominant Theme
## – Opinions on the Lantern Festival Lyrics by Li Qingzhao, Liu Chenweng and Wang Yuanliang

Miao Yue

The Lantern Festival falls on the 15th day of the first month in the lunar calendar and has been the festival for enjoying lanterns since ancient times. There are quite a few poetry on the Lantern Festival, and most are joyful pieces. The renowned works are as follows. The *Lantern Festival Night* by Su Weidao of the Tang Dynasty reads:

*"The light is bright, tonight the no-go area is opening.
The horse gallop that stirred up the dust, the moon*

*seemed to follow the people.*
*The young singing girls look more beautiful, they*
*walk and sing songs.*
*The capital guards does not work tonight, the drum*
*will not urge the people back home."*

And the first stanza of the *Lantern Festival Night* to the tune of *Green Jade Cup* by Xin Qiji reads:

*"One night's east wind adorns a thousand trees with*
*flowers*
*And blows down stars in showers.*
*Fine steeds and carved cabs spread fragrance en route;*
*Music vibrates from the flute;*
*The moon sheds its full light*
*While fish and dragon lanterns dance all night."*

In addition to the numerous joyful verses, there are several Lantern Festival works which are pervasive with a sorrowful mood and compliant with Yu Xin's view of "Sorrow is the dominant theme instead of description on bitterness" in the *Preface to the Sighs at Southern China*. The reason is that poets experiencing dramatic changes and national crises often pondered on the country's destiny and individual fates, especially on the occasion of festival seasons and days. The Lantern Festival lyrics by Li Qingzhao, Liu Chenweng and Wang Yuanliang of the

Song Dynasty belong to this kind. In comparison with the works on pleasant festivals, their verses are more moving. Now, let's try to comment.

First, let's appreciate Li Qingzhao's work.

### Tune: Joy of Eternal Union

*The setting sun like molten gold*
*Gathering clouds like marble cold,*
*Where is my dear,*
*Willows take misty dye,*
*Flutes for mume blossoms sigh.*
*Can you say spring is here?*
*On the Lantern Festival*
*The weather is agreeable.*
*Will wind and rain not come again?*
*I thank my friends in verse and wine,*
*With scented cabs and horses fine*
*Coming to invite me in vain.*

*I remember the pleasure*
*Ladies enjoyed at leisure*
*In the capital on this day:*
*Headdress with emerald*
*And filigree of gold*
*Vied in fashion display.*
*Now with a languid air*
*And disheveled frosty hair*
*I dare not go out in the evening.*

*I'd rather forward lean*
*Behind the window screen*
*To hear the others' laughter ring.*

According to Zhang Duanyi's record, the lyric was composed by Li Qingzhao in her late years for recalling the bygones in the capital. Li Qingzhao really experienced dramatic changes. In 1127, the Jin State terminated the Northern Song and captured the emperors. In 1129, Zhao Mingcheng, husband of Li Qingzhao, died of illness. Then, the Jin troops crossed the Yangtze River to attack the Southern Song. Li Qingzhao had to flee around to elude the war in the southern region. In 1136, she finally returned to Lin'an (the capital of Southern Song, today's Hangzhou). She suffered seriously from the ten-year-long exile and the national and family miseries. So, in a Lantern Festival evening, Li composed the lyric in Lin'an, the capital of Southern Song, to recall the joyful celebration of the festival in Bianjing, the capital of Northern Song.

The first stanza describes the "On the Lantern Festival/The weather is agreeable." But the lyricist had no mood and refused the grand invitation of her friends: "I thank my friends in verse and wine,/With scented cabs and horses fine/Coming to invite me in vain." The second stanza starts with the recollection on the Lantern Festival celebration in the peaceful and prosperous capital Bianjing: "I remember the pleasure/Ladies enjoyed at leisure/In the capital on this day:/Headdress with emerald/And filigree of gold/Vied in fashion display." Then come the powerful lines on the reality to depict the low mood and the trauma of wars: "Now with a languid air/And disheveled frosty hair/I dare not go out in the evening." The ending lines "I'd rather forward lean/Behind the window screen/To hear the others' laughter ring" vivify the lyricist's loneliness and desolation. To sum up, Li Qingzhao expressed her deep sorrow over the vicissitudes of the country and her family through the ode to the Lantern Festival.

One hundred years later after the lyric, Liu Chenweng, adherents of the Southern Song, composed two lyrics on the Lantern Festival to the tune *Joy of Eternal Union and Appearance of a Precious Cauldron* to express his grief over the lost country. Let's first come to his *Joy of Eternal Union*:

### Tune: Joy of Eternal Union

*Since the Lantern Festival of the Yihai Year (1275), I have been reading the touching lyric Joy of Eternal Union by Li Qingzhao for three years. I could not control my mood when reading Li's verse and composed a lyric to the same tune. Even my talent is less competitive than Li, my grief is more intense than hers.*

*The moon has just shown her face shining like a round piece of jade,*

*Thinning clouds fade and drift away, who springtime dominates?*
*In the palatial garden wintriness lingers, by the lake warmth wears me out,*
*As bygones flash before my eyes.*
*Among the grass is fragrant dust, bright lanterns light the night,*
*More often I've grown lazy, no mood to go out side by side.*
*Yet how could anyone have known that on this night of no fire and light,*
*This town would melancholy seem as if it is enduring a storm.*

*In the old days of Xuanhe, the capital had been moved across waters to Lin'an,*
*Pretty was the scenery and things were much the same.*
*Turning the pages of volumes and volumes of literature at the windy Lantern Festival time,*
*Those who compose verses suffer the most.*
*There is no place to take refuge in southern China like Du Fu's night in Fuzhou,*
*The bitterness he suffered, who really knows how to cope?*
*In vain I face the dimming lamp wide awake,*
*All over the village resonates the drumming of the Shrine Day alike.*

Liu Chenweng (1232-1297), alias Huimeng, was a native of Luling (today's Ji'an of Jiangxi province). He was the disciple of Lu Xiangshan as a candidate for the highest academy of learning. He offended Jia Sidao, the treacherous premier, at the imperial examination and was ranked low. He applied for the management of Lianxi Academy to care for his parents. After the Southern Song Dynasty collapsed, he also passed away in seclusion. In 1274, the year prior to the lyric, the Yuan troops captured Xiangyang and attacked southward. The Southern Song was in an extremely precarious situation. Liu foresaw the upcoming disasters and his similar destiny with Li Qingzhao. As expected, the Yuan troops captured Lin'an and the Emperor Gongdi in 1276, and Zhao Shi, the last emperor of Southern Song, were driven to the sea in 1279, marking the complete failure of Song's rejuvenation. Thus, Liu ended the lyric in tragic lines: "There is no place to take refuge in southern China like Du Fu's night in Fuzhou,/The bitterness he suffered, who really knows how to cope?/In vain I face the dimming lamp wide awake,/All over the village resonates the drumming of the Shrine Day alike." The situation in this lyric of Liu is even worse than that in Li Qingzhao's as the fragmentary Southern Song still existed in Li's lyric, but completely collapsed when Liu composed the verse. On the Lantern Festival of 1297, two decades after the Song's termination, Liu composed a lyric to the melody of *Appearance of a Precious Cauldron* to recall the prosperity of the former capitals on Lantern Festival and mourn for the past dynasty. The lyric is partly quoted as follows:

"Dressed in red for a ride in spring,
We galloped under the moon over shadows of poles
and banners through the city.
I cannot see an end to the dancing and singing taking
place on balconies,
Where lively lotus trot fragrant dust raises.
The music of flutes has stopped inviting the bright
phoenixes to rise homeward,
There is no fear of the golden vanguards falling
intoxicated.
I wonder why along the imperial avenue the hustle
and bustle would die away
When the songs reminiscent of the charm of a Tang
songstress are performed.

Those a generation before us still remember the
Xuanhe days,
Holding a bronze dew plate gathering tears crystal
clear like water.
...
I think of getting in front of a lamp to my hair comb,
Yet I end up crying pearls under the rose.
Even if I had ever seen with my own eyes the dance of
the Rainbow Robe,
A heavenly memory as such on earth I could only in
dreams evoke."

The aforesaid lyrics on Lantern Festival by Li Qingzhao and Liu Chenweng have won great popularity and been passed on for generations. The other lyric on Lantern Festival composed by Wang Yuanliang is comparable with the aforesaid two, but hasn't received attention it deserves. Now, let's have a look at the piece by Wang Yuanliang, a lyricist suddenly rose in the transient period of Song and Yuan dynasties.

**Tune: Message to Jade Maiden**
*Lantern Festival after the Downfall of the Song Dynasty*

*Who would enjoy any more the delight*
*Of splendid lantern night?*
*Moonlit bowers and flowery pavilions*
*Disappeared in the dust.*
*All prosperity vanished*
*Except green mountains still stood.*
*In the bright moonlight capital*
*We only see the tide rise and fall.*
*Dots on dots of lantern light*
*Feel shame to see the dancer fair and songstress bright,*
*Mume blossoms look like jade,*
*Before the Lord of Spring they fade.*
*The princess sheds tear on tear,*
*Playing on pipa strings in fear.*
*If you will know her parting grief forlon,*
*Just listen in watchtower to the dreary horn!*

Wang Yuanliang, alias Dayou or Shuiyun, was a native of Qiantang (today's Hangzhou). His poetry were collected in *Sketches of Lake and Mountain Types (Hu Shan Lei Gao)*. Born in 1241, he had served for the court due to his zither skill in his youthhood. In the spring of 1276, the Yuan troops captured Lin'an and took captive the emperor, the queen and the concubines. Wang and the captives were taken to the north where Wang had a hard time. He also visited the imprisoned Wen Tianxiang several times and composed poems with the prisoner. After Wen was executed, Wang composed nine elegies for him. In 1288, Wang returned back to the south. And in 1294, he started a seclusive life by the Western Lake in Hangzhou. He died in late 1317.

According to Kong Fanli, the *Message to Jade Maiden* was written on the Lantern Festival of 1276, the eve of the Yuan's capture of Hangzhou. In 1274, the Yuan troops attack southward. The next year, the invaders captured cities along the Yangtze River including Jiankang (Nanjing) and Pingjiang (Suzhou). On the Lantern Festival of 1276, Wang foresaw the downfall of Song and sighed "All prosperity vanished/Except green mountains still stood./In the bright moonlight capital/We only see the tide rise and fall." Despite of the festival, the lyricist was in a low mood and felt pervasive bleakness: "Dots on dots of lantern light/Feel shame to see the dancer fair and songstress bright,/Mume blossoms look like jade,/Before the Lord of Spring they fade./The princess sheds tear on tear,/Playing on pipa strings in fear."

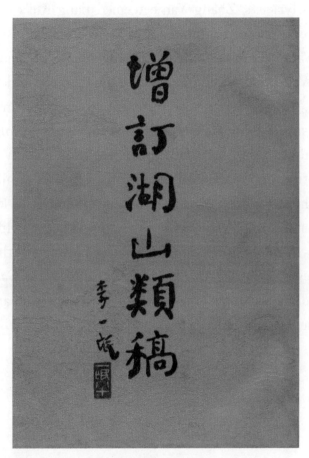

Photocopy of *Revised Sketches of Lake and
Mountain Types (Hu Shan Lei Gao)*

Wang Yuanliang featured a unique style. At the end of Song Dynasty and early Yuan Dynasty, Jiang Kui and Wu Wenying were leaders in southern China. Of the then famous lyricists, Zhang Yan esteemed Jiang Kui's style of freshness, Zhou Mi imitated Wu Wenying's exquisiteness and Wang Yisun assimilated the advantages of Jiang and Wu. Wang had no contact with Zhang, Zhou and Wang Yisun. Wang's lyrics, also different from others in style, express his emotion straightforward with simple and plain diction in a graceful mode. He didn't apply many quotations or elaborate depictions. He was similar to Liu Chenweng in lyric style. After returning back from the north, Wang visited Liu in Luling. They felt like old friends at the first meeting. Liu prefaced Wang's anthology *Sketches of Lake and Mountain Types (Hu Shan Lei Gao)* and praised his accomplishments because of their similarity in experiences and lyric style.

An Elegy to the Life
– On *Courtyard Full of Fragrance*
by Xu Junbao's Wife

Zang Kejia

### Tune: Courtyard Full of Fragrance

*The prosperity along the Hanshui River,*
*The elite in the Southern China,*
*Have inherited the charming tradition of the past*
*years.*
*Along a five kilometer-long street, flowery windows*
*and vermilion doors,*
*Are dotted with dazzling curtain hooks*

*Once the war broke out*
*The flags flew*
*Millions of Mongolian troops will sweep through*
*Performance bowers and chambers*
*Which are like fallen pedals in storm.*

*The three-century-long peace, the achievements and*
*the celebrities*
*Make an end with the lost land.*
*Fortunately, I am not captured to the northward,*
*And still in the south I reside.*
*Where are you, my husband!*
*In vain I am in great sorrow*
*Without an excuse to see you.*
*From now on, every night,*
*My soul will fly homeward to you.*

I am fond of classical poetry and the Song lyrics in particular. I have been reading various classical anthologies to seek for a spiritual delight. I am familiar with works of renowned masters. But I nearly neglect the *Courtyard Full of Fragrance (Prosperity of Hanshang)*, a masterpiece by a female lyricist. I regret not to have read this great verse before. The authoress didn't enjoy a high reputation like other female lyricists. She only had this verse passed on to later generations and was remembered as Xu Junbao's Wife in literati. The lyric has an extremely high artistic value, showcasing the intense patriotism and faithfulness in love of a girl.

The lyric, just like a pearl, gives out brilliant splendor to enlighten the writer and the readers. The more times I read the lyric, the more excited I will be. It makes me remember the noted works on indignation by Cai Yan, the female poet living at the end of Han Dynasty, by Wang Qinghui and Wang Yuanliang, the contemporaries of the authoress. Different from others' living on in degradation, the authoress selected a decent death. Her brave choice at the life-and-death moment was solemn and stirring.

The downfall of Southern Song is a great tragedy of the nation and people caused by the corruption of the rulers. The authoress of the *Courtyard Full of Fragrance* was just a minor character in the tragedy. In the lyric, the lyricist summarized the tragic death of the Southern Song with her intense sorrow and skillful artistic expression. The termination of the Southern Song, like a sudden collapse of a dazzling jade tower, made people feel sorrowful, indignant and commiserative. The most tragic in the lyric is that the lyricist experienced a sudden fall from the prosperity to the reality and saw the attack of the enemy in a panic. Even in a closed boudoir, she should have some knowledge about the state affairs, the dispute between the capitulationists and the war party and other critical events. But she was intoxicated by the capitulation atmosphere and enjoyed singing and dancing. To understand the lyric, we should read the records on the historical background, such as *Xuanhe Anecdotes (Xuan*

*He Yi Shi)*, *Dreams of Bianliang (Dong Jing Meng Hua Lu)*, *Records on Prosperity (Fan Sheng Lu)*, *Records of Bianliang (Meng Liang Lu)*, *Interests of Capital (Du Cheng Ji Sheng)* and *Old Tales of Wulin (Wu Lin Jiu Shi)*, to have a complete knowledge on the absurd dreams, the tragic scenes and the complicated mood of the authoress. Then, we can know why the authoress still recalled the "prosperity along the Hanshui River." The prosperity is actually a toxic and enchanted mushroom which poisoned the people. The so-called "elite in the Southern China" include the dissolute emperor and the treacherous officials who destroyed the country and the people. "Along a five kilometer-long street, flowery windows and vermilion doors,/Are dotted with dazzling curtain hooks" are descriptions of the deluxe life to serve as a foil for the ignorance of the enemy's approaching attack. The situation was like the depiction in the lines "The soft and drowsy breeze the wandering throng enchants. /Hangzhou, the new-found capital, their old Bianzhou supplants." Then come the unavoidable results "Millions of Mongolian troops will sweep through/ Performance bowers and chambers/Which are like fallen pedals in storm."

The lyric starts with recollection of the bygones. Then comes to the cruel reality. At the end, the lyricist showed her deep sorrow and yearning for the peace, elite and bygones. The lyric reflects the tragedy of the times and the lyricist herself. The sincere emotion and poor situation

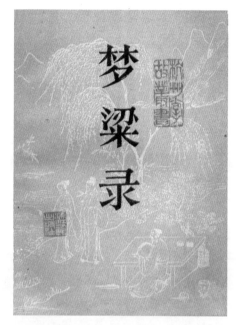

Photocopy of *Dreams of Bianliang*
*(Dong Jing Meng Hua Lu)*

Photocopy of *Records of Bianliang*
*(Meng Liang Lu)*

of the lyricist are the source of the moving verse. She was both a weak dreamer and a strong realist. The moving lines "Fortunately, I am not captured to the northward, /And still in the south I reside" can easily arouse the readers' resonance and pity.

"And yearn for boundless land which fades! /Easy to leave it but hard to see it again." The lyricist was heartbroken at the termination of the country and the death of her husband. After composing the elegy to life, she left the world forever.

**图书在版编目（CIP）数据**

名家讲宋词:英文/《文史知识》编辑部编;朱建廷,赵国亚译.
-- 北京:五洲传播出版社, 2016.1
（中国文化经典导读）
ISBN 978-7-5085-3319-3

Ⅰ.①名… Ⅱ.①文… ②创… Ⅲ.①宋词－诗词研究－英文 Ⅳ.①I207.23

中国版本图书馆CIP数据核字(2016)第023154号


编　　者：《文史知识》编辑部
翻　　译：朱建廷　赵国亚
出 版 人：荆孝敏
责任编辑：苏　谦
装帧设计：宋　雪




**名家讲宋词**

出版发行：五洲传播出版社
地　　址：北京市海淀区北三环中路31号生产力大楼B座6层（100088）
电　　话：010-82005927，010-82007837
网　　址：www.cicc.org.cn　　e-mail：liuyang@cicc.org.cn

出　　版：中华书局
地　　址：北京市丰台区太平桥西里38号（100073）
网　　址：http://www.zhbc.com.cn　　e-mail：zhbc@zhbc.com.cn

印　　刷：北京利丰雅高长城印刷有限公司
开　　本：155×230毫米　1/16
印　　张：15
字　　数：150千字
版　　次：2016年3月第1版第1次印刷
定　　价：129.00元